The Mind Trap

Also by G. Clifton Wisler

The Antrian Messenger
The Seer

Piper's Ferry
The Wolf's Tooth
The Raid
Buffalo Moon
Thunder on the Tennessee
Winter of the Wolf
Esmeralda
Lakota
Ross's Gap
The Return of Caulfield Blake
This New Land
Antelope Springs
The Trident Brand
A Cry of Angry Thunder
My Brother, the Wind

The Mind Trap

G. Clifton Wisler

LODESTAR BOOKS

Dutton   New York

Copyright © 1990 by G. Clifton Wisler

Library of Congress Cataloging-in-Publication Data

Wisler, G. Clifton.
    The mind trap / G. Clifton Wisler.—1st ed.
        p.   cm.
    Summary: Scott's identity as a telepathic alien from another
planet may be exposed when he's imprisoned in a research institute for
psychic children run by a mysterious doctor.
    ISBN 0-525-67464-0
    [1. Extrasensory perception—Fiction.   2. Extraterrestrial beings—
Fiction.   3. Science fiction.]   I. Title.
PZ7.W78033Mi   1990
[Fic]—dc20   90-6542
                                                                        CIP
                                                                         AC

Published in the United States by Lodestar Books,
an affiliate of Dutton Children's Books,
a division of Penguin Books USA Inc.

Editor: Rosemary Brosnan

Printed in the U.S.A.
First Edition
10   9   8   7   6   5   4

for stargazers and dreamers everywhere

The Mind Trap

1

Dallas that April was a world of sunshine and color. Acres of thick, green grass danced beneath clear, bright-blue skies. In between, budding dogwoods and long beds of roses splashed pinks and whites and yellows. It was a dazzling scene, a land reawakening from winter's slumber.

Scott drank it in like a wayfarer staggering across a barren desert. He breathed the scent of fresh-clipped lawns and tasted honeysuckle growing on fences. Spring had come like an old friend to welcome him, it seemed.

"Why not?" he whispered as he scanned the large viewing screen in the ship's control room. "It's my birthday, isn't it?"

Concentrating harder on the screen, he projected himself on that distant hillside, tossing Frisbees or racing bicycles with other teenagers. On the far side of a large lake two boys not much older than himself were dueling on a tennis court as admiring friends looked on.

He shifted the screen a hundred yards and found a family gathering around a picnic table. Farther on, a pack of Cub

Scouts sailed wooden boats. Beyond them, pale sailboats cut across the azure water, carried along like soaring eagles by a gentle breeze.

"I should be out there," he mumbled.

"Scott?" a deep, thoughtful voice called.

Scott guiltily swept the screen clear and scrambled to his feet as the heavy metal hatch opened. Tiaf entered slowly.

"You know it's not necessary to close off these compartments when we're stationary," the white-haired old man said as he secured the hatch.

"I . . . just . . ."

"Needed to be alone?" Tiaf asked.

Scott shook his head, but his eyes attested to the lie. Tiaf raised an eyebrow and motioned toward the blank screen.

"You miss them still?" Tiaf asked.

"Always will, I suppose," Scott said, sighing. "Especially today."

Tiaf appeared momentarily confused. Scott frowned and started to speak, but Tiaf's eyes urged silence.

"Yes, I see now," Tiaf said, gazing as familiar scenes began crossing the viewing screen. One birthday memory after another appeared, and Scott alternately laughed and sighed. Finally the screen filled with a solemn hillside topped by small metal plaques and larger monuments of marble or granite. Near a plaque marked SCOTT CHILDERS a yellow-haired boy of thirteen huddled with his parents. Beside them a teenage girl sobbed.

"He would've been fifteen today, Mom," the boy said, running his fingers along the cold, dew-spattered rim of the plaque. "Bet he'd have gotten tall this year."

"Maybe," the woman answered, squeezing the hands of her son and husband.

2

"He worried about that some," the boy continued. "Don't know why. You'd think anybody as smart as Scott wouldn't care about being tall."

"He worried about everything," the girl said, swallowing her sadness momentarily. "But mostly he worried about us. He saved us, after all."

"Yeah," the boy said, dropping his eyes toward the ground.

Scott paled as he read the pain etched on their faces. His mother and father—he couldn't think of them as anything else—seemed tormented. Sharon, too. And young Brian . . . he looked so lost!

"Was I right, Tiaf, to let them believe me dead?" Scott asked. "You said the sadness would pass, but it hasn't."

"Who can understand Earthers?" Tiaf asked, placing a wrinkled hand on the boy's shoulder. "I've been among them so long, but they remain a mystery."

"You're an observer, Tiaf. You visit sometimes, passing on your warnings. But I was one of them. For fourteen years."

"Yes, you were born of another world, but it was here you first walked, first talked, first saw and felt and knew. You are a Zhyposian and a seer, my young friend, but you have Earther instincts, too."

"That's not bad, is it?" Scott asked as he touched the rough edge of the viewing screen with his fingers, hoping somehow that part of the warmth he saw there might flow through him.

"Not bad," Tiaf said as he rubbed the tension from Scott's shoulders. "Different, though. Confusing. And perhaps dangerous."

"For whom?"

3

"Everyone," Tiaf said, taking his place in the pilot's seat alongside Scott. "You want to go back to them. You think you can ease their pain. You can't. Listen to their thoughts. Hear them. And remember that last day."

Scott closed his eyes and focused his mind on the distant faces of his family and friends. Sharon's mind swam with dozens of recollections—capsizing a paddleboat at the sixth-grade party, tripping each other at the freshman dance! Scott read longing, but he saw other boys in her thoughts, too. She had a movie date with Roger Brantley that very night.

"Didn't figure she'd join a convent," Scott remarked.

"And your family?" Tiaf asked.

Scott heard his parents sharing memories of a child adopted as their own, raised with love and concern, yet remaining different. And Brian? He was growing like a weed! But it was Brian who most concerned Scott.

Through the thirteen-year-old's memory paraded the terrible events that had led to Scott's departure from the world he knew and loved. First the investigators had come. Then they'd returned to take Scott away. He'd escaped to Tiaf, only to have a vision of a terrible school-bus accident—and Sharon and Brian dying. So Scott Childers had returned to save them and vanish into the rain-swollen creek instead. It had seemed so, anyway.

Don't feel guilty, Brian, Scott silently urged. *I'm fine. Take care of them, and yourself, too.*

"Mom, Dad, it happened again!" Brian announced. "I heard Scott speaking. Like a ghost or something!"

"Brian, that's nonsense," their father declared. "It's just your grief talking."

"Maybe," the boy said, brightening. "But I never did

believe anybody who knew about things happening ahead of time, who could just up and appear on that road like magic, couldn't pop out of that car and save himself. Maybe that's how he can talk to me."

"That's enough of that!" Mr. Childers said, glancing around nervously. "It's impossible, of course, but probably very dangerous to even hint at such things. You wouldn't want those men coming back, asking more questions, would you, Brian?"

"Brian, honey, you remember seeing Scott's body, don't you?" Mrs. Childers said, trembling as she gripped the wrists of her younger son. "I wanted to believe he got away too, but . . ."

"Sure," Brian said, nodding. But he wasn't convinced.

I heard you, Scotty. I'll look after them, Brian thought.

Scott froze. Invisible fingers seemed to tear at him.

"Tiaf, it's not possible, is it? Brian being telepathic, I mean."

"It's not him," Tiaf assured Scott. "You simply are growing stronger. A seer can do many things. Among them he can implant an idea or transmit a message."

"You mean I could tell Mom and Dad things, too? And Sharon?"

"You transmitted the image of your body in the casket, didn't you? As for implanting an idea, it would require a mind receptive to your voice."

"You mean somebody ready to believe what he's hearing."

"That's it, partly. Such a mind must feel a certain kinship with you. And the mind itself must possess certain capacities."

"You mean the person has to be partly telepathic?"

"Oh, Earthers are a long way from developing their small

latent talents. They dabble in parlor tricks and call it science. If a man guesses the suit of a playing card, he is a mentalist. To receive a message, a mind must open itself to possibilities. That's rare among Earthers."

"But possible?"

"Throughout the ages there have been powerful human minds. They're rarely cultivated, though. Once, these people were burned as witches or deemed mad. The lucky ones learn to conceal their abilities."

"And Brian?"

"Hungers for your words. And so he hears."

"I hear him, too, Tiaf. Before, I never heard anybody but you."

"You always had the ability, Scott," Tiaf explained. "As I told you once before, the hard thing is not hearing. The challenge is to channel, so that your mind isn't battered by all manner of random thoughts."

Scott nodded, then took a long final look at the screen before clearing it.

"Yes, you could visit them," Tiaf said, reading Scott's thoughts. "But you heard your father. It would be perilous for them as well as for you. It hasn't been so long—"

"Half a year now," Scott interrupted. "How many places have we been in that time? How many centuries? I've seen a hundred countries, watched Roman legions march, seen Troy fall, even helped build an Egyptian temple. Remember that?"

"I recall everything, Scott. And a thousand places I have been besides."

"Don't you get tired of it?"

"Why? Don't you learn something each time? I warned you. I come as a guide—a teacher."

6

"A student's due a holiday every once in a while, though, isn't he, Tiaf? Even in Zhypos, they must have given kids a day off once in a while."

"And this being the anniversary of your birth . . ."

"I won't go home, Tiaf. It probably *is* dangerous. But earlier I was looking at a park. Right here in Dallas. There's a bike trail around it. People playing tennis and softball, sailing and picnicking . . ."

"You'll be cautious?"

"I promise. And if there's even a hint of trouble, I'll grasp my ring, duck behind a tree, and *poof!*"

"The Earther instinct is strong," Tiaf observed as Scott projected the park on the viewing screen. "Ah, the girls."

Scott's face reddened as a gang of teenage girls whizzed past on bicycles.

"It's my birthday," Scott explained. "Just happens once a year, after all."

"Be careful," Tiaf urged.

"I promise," Scott said, raising his right hand. He gazed in dismay at his simple cotton tunic and trousers. Instantly he transposed them into a pair of blue-jean cutoffs and a white tank top. Scott gave his pale flesh a bronze tint. Then he stared hard at the bright emerald set in the brass base of an ancient ring. The stone began to glow, and Scott felt himself growing warm as molecules became excited. One minute he sat in the control room. The next he was whirling through time and space. He reassembled near a stone shelter in the lakeside park. And when he stepped out from hiding, he was nearly run down by the very bicyclists he had seen on the screen.

"Better watch where you walk around here," a dark-haired girl about his own age warned. "These cyclists will run you over in a hurry."

"Yeah?" Scott asked, following the girl toward the lakeshore. "Guess you come here often."

"No, almost never," she said, frowning. "School and all. I keep pretty busy. How about you?"

"First time," Scott confessed. "Truth is, I've only been to Dallas a couple of times, and then just overnight."

"Visiting relatives on spring break, I guess. I used to do that. I'm Gigi," she said, smiling.

"I'm Scott. I'm here with my uncle," he added, using the old cover story Tiaf recommended. "This place reminds me some of Central Park in New York, though. Lots of grass and people. Right in the heart of the city."

"You've been to New York?" she asked. "I've always wanted to go there. To the Met especially."

"I don't think much of opera myself," Scott remarked.

"Not the opera." She laughed. "The Metropolitan Museum. It has just about the finest exhibits of Egyptian art in the country, you know. Maybe in the world."

"I did know," Scott said. He was half tempted to reveal a touch of what else he knew about Egyptian art, but he recalled Tiaf's words: *Be cautious!*

"Have you had lunch?" the girl asked. "We're having a picnic and brought plenty of food."

"Oh?"

"Yeah. Look," she added, pointing to a cluster of youngsters dressed in identical green shorts and yellow shirts with white stripes. There was just one other girl, and except for a pair of older boys and a scholarly-looking man, most of the kids were in their early teens.

"Your school?" he asked.

8

"We're sort of a special academy. Gifted kids. You know, weird and all."

"Oh, sure," Scott said, following her toward the others. A pair of identical-looking ten-year-olds were tossing a Frisbee with a slightly older boy, and Scott retrieved an errant toss for them.

"I brought a friend for lunch," the girl called. "That okay?"

"Sure, Gigi!" a tall woman Scott hadn't noticed before answered. "Corral Grant there, will you?"

A dark-haired boy who had been tossing the Frisbee with the twins seemed to be straying, and Gigi motioned Scott toward a nearby parking lot that formed the unofficial boundary of the Frisbee field. As Scott headed that way, he was suddenly struck by an odd sensation. Then voices seemed to flood his thoughts. He was hearing them all—the twins plotting against their companion, an older boy's appraisal of a pair of female sunbathers, even the scholarly-looking gentleman worrying about some project.

The words were swept from Scott's mind by something else—a burning sensation. Instantly he clasped his forehead in an effort to ease the pain. He shuddered.

"Hey, you all right?" Gigi called.

Scott fought through the chaos and focused on the beginnings of a vision. The parking lot appeared, quiet as before. Then a car roared out of nowhere. The Frisbee flew through the air, and the little dark-haired scamp dashed between a Ford van and a Dodge pickup. His hands reached for the flying red disk, but a speeding convertible slammed into him first. Scott heard only a trace of a scream, and then . . .

"You all right?" Gigi asked again as she shook Scott back to consciousness.

"Sure," he told her. "I guess it . . . maybe the heat . . ."

"Yeah. Hey, Grant, see if you can find my friend here a Coke, will you?"

"Ah, Gigi," the dark-haired boy complained. "Can't somebody else do it? It's my picnic, you know."

"I'll do it myself," she grumbled, leading Scott toward a collection of food baskets and ice chests. She handed him a Coke and took one herself.

"Thanks," he told her.

"Sure. Help yourself to some food. Ever play any tennis? Jay and Geoff challenged me to a set of doubles, and Grant's supposed to be my partner. He'd rather spend the afternoon on a paddleboat, though."

"He your brother?" Scott asked.

"Cousin. But in a way we're all sort of family here."

He gazed out at the Frisbee players again. He couldn't help grinning as he listened to their thoughts. So many pranks and adventures lurked there. Well, why not? The sun was bright, and the air was ripe for foolishness.

Then the vision returned. Scott closed his eyes and tried to shake it off, but the images persisted. Little Grant raced toward the parking lot, his mind cluttered with daydreams. *It's my birthday!* the boy thought again and again. Then he froze as he spied the onrushing convertible.

"His birthday?" Scott whispered as he reopened his eyes.

"Yeah," Gigi said, gazing up in surprise. "How'd you know? He just turned twelve."

The twins began working the Frisbee back toward the parking lot then, and a car swerved around a pair of cyclists and raced into the parking lot, honking its horn wildly. Scott leaped to his feet and flew across the park. He had never run so fast in his entire life. He hurdled a bench

10

and dashed past a surprised couple as he hurried to help. The Frisbee was already airborne, though, and . . .

The convertible tried to stop. Its brakes screeched, and it swerved, smashing the side of a Buick station wagon and splintering a small cottonwood before careening onward. Scott managed in that split second to capture Grant and shove him behind the van. The convertible skidded on.

"Tiaf?" Scott whispered as he grasped his ring. There wasn't time, though. The big car struck, knocking Scott down, then under. Pain exploded through him as bones snapped. It seemed for a moment as if Scott might simply dissolve, for his insides were battered and shaken. He tried to grasp the ring again, but his fingers wouldn't move. He was frozen. Then a wave of agony swept over him, and he screamed.

2

Scott awoke in a white cloud. At least that was what it seemed to be at first glance. Gradually, as his vision sharpened, he detected distinct shapes. The place had walls, corners, a door, and one window with a heavy metal frame. It wasn't the ship, though. Everything here was square. The walls met at right angles. The ship was rounded. Even the bunks had curves to them.

He lay in a large, chrome-trimmed bed. Overhead was a steel framework from which dangled a trapezelike bar. Transparent tubes drew mysterious liquids from plastic sacks into his left wrist. Every inch of the place, from the sheets to the linen curtains over the window, was ivory white and sanitized.

It's a hospital! Scott realized.

Pieces of the accident came back to him. He recalled lying in the street, his body bent and broken. People looked down at him with wide, curious eyes. A pair of teenagers argued with a park policeman.

"It's all my fault," Grant explained. "He pushed me out of the way, but he couldn't—"

"He knew!" Gigi exclaimed.

"He's not dead," the scholarly-looking man announced as he motioned the onlookers back.

"Has he got parents here?" a second policeman asked. "Anybody know him?"

"He's got an uncle," Gigi said as she calmed Grant. "He told me so."

"We'll need to notify—" the policeman began.

"No, I'll take responsibility," the scholarly-looking man announced. "I'm a doctor."

"Yes, sir, but I still have to call an ambulance," the officer argued. "We have our procedures."

"Call this number," the doctor barked, drawing a card from his pocket and plunging it into the policeman's hand. "Iris, when is that fool Malin getting the ambulance here?"

Scott's memory began to blur then. He knew he'd been carried on a stretcher into some strange kind of long van, but afterward everything was hazy. Mostly he remembered pain. He'd never been hurt so badly before, and it was a new sensation. Every inch of him ached. One leg remained numb, and he couldn't move the fingers of his left hand.

Well, Tiaf, I've done it this time! Scott thought. Strangely though, Tiaf didn't answer. Always before, the two of them had been able to communicate no matter what the distance. Perhaps the injuries had affected him, though.

Scott lifted his chin and swallowed the resulting pain. He really was a mess. Both legs were encased in plaster from the hips down. His midsection was wrapped in a steel corset, and his left shoulder and arm were strapped in place by an assortment of fiberglass and nylon straps. Each breath brought fresh waves of agony. Concentrating with great intensity, Scott's eyes bored past the bandages and saw the damaged ligaments and shattered bones. The convertible had done serious internal damage—enough perhaps to bring death. Treatment so far had brought only temporary repairs. The spleen and one kidney were particularly bad.

Scott had little experience as a healer. He'd mended broken bones, but this was far more difficult. He recalled Tiaf's teachings, though. *Reconstitute them. Think of them as they were before, and it will be so.* Scott did it just that way. First he remolded the spleen. He could feel a comforting warmth spread through him. He made right the torn and abused fabric of the kidney. Broken blood vessels and strained cartilage became whole. Finally he concentrated hard on his fractured ribs. Bone knitted itself until at last he was able to breathe with ease.

Thereafter he lay quite still for a time. The effort left him empty, totally exhausted. An hour later he gathered the strength to repair a broken wrist and the crushed fingers of his left hand. He was repairing the last of the metatarsal breaks when the door opened.

"He's awake," Gigi cried somewhat triumphantly. "I told you."

"Yeah, he's better," Grant added, balancing a large food tray awkwardly as he entered the room. "Doc said you'd sleep another whole day, but Gigi knew you'd come to."

"She did?" Scott asked, looking nervously at the self-assured girl.

"She always knows these kinds of things," Grant explained. "Reads minds."

"Do not," Gigi insisted as she located a rolling table and adjusted it so that it hung over Scott's bed. "I just study medical books. Twenty-four hours is usually the full duration of unconsciousness when the patient hasn't suffered head trauma."

"Twenty-four hours?" Scott asked. "I've been here a whole day?"

"Day and a half," Gigi explained. "It's already past dinner. We had to bribe Malin so we could smuggle this food to you."

"That was pretty stupid," Grant said, pointing to the intravenous tubes attached to Scott's hand. "They're feeding him fluids, Gigi. You heard Doc say his ribs were busted. I bet he can't even swallow."

"Doctors make mistakes," Scott explained as he pulled the needles from his hand.

"Scott!" Gigi objected.

"I feel just fine, and I'm ready for some real food," Scott told his worried companions. "You understand, don't you?"

He painted a mental picture of mending bones and patched organs, and Gigi's face grew pale.

"You don't understand," Grant said, frowning. "Doc says they'll have to bring in somebody and operate."

"No, I'm feeling better by the minute," Scott said, making the effort to sit up.

"Here," Gigi said, reaching for a knob on the side of the bed. The entire back half began to rise with a hum, and soon Scott found himself propelled into a sitting position. "Better?" she asked.

"Doc'll skin us for sure now," Grant said, anxiously eyeing the open door. "We could make it worse, Gigi, stirring up his insides and all. And maybe he needs the medicines in those tubes!"

"No, I'm fine," Scott said, reassuring them. "Help me get

15

out of this harness, will you? I can barely move my left arm."

"It's broken," Gigi said, stopping him. "Your hand's in bad shape, too. I guess it was . . ."

"It's fine," Scott declared as he flexed his fingers. "Doctors don't know everything."

She stared in amazement at the rebuilt fingers, then helped Scott remove the braces. Once freed of the apparatus, Scott eased himself into a comfortable position and started in on the food. He was starved. Even the bland beef patty and carrots tasted good to him.

"I can't believe it," Gigi said when he swallowed the final scrap of bread. "Your arm. It's not even bruised."

"I'm a fast healer," Scott told her.

"But I saw those fingers myself," she cried. "It's just not possible."

"Oh, you'd be surprised what's possible," he said, grinning.

"No, not around this place," Grant said, nudging Gigi. "We better go now."

"You need your rest," Gigi added. "We'll be back in the morning for a visit. Can we bring you anything?"

"No, I'll be fine," Scott replied. *And elsewhere*, he thought. Gigi's face paled as he spoke. Then she grabbed the tray and motioned Grant along, and the two of them made their escape down the narrow corridor.

Scott watched them through the doorway for half a minute. They vanished from view all too quickly, though. He returned the bed to its horizontal position and prepared to mend his legs. That was when the scholarly-looking man appeared in the doorway.

"Well, you look a good deal better," he declared. "We

16

were quite concerned. I'm Dr. Victor Edgefield. I've been overseeing your treatment."

"Why's that?" Scott asked, reading something unspoken in the doctor's mind.

"Well, that was the least I could do," the doctor answered. "You saved my boy's life, after all. We all worried about you. It was a great shame you were so badly hurt, and if we'd left things to the police, they would have had you scribbling forms while you bled to death."

"Am I in a private hospital of some kind?"

"In a way," Dr. Edgefield said, noticing for the first time the discarded shoulder brace. "What in the world? Who did that?"

The doctor turned to summon help when Scott raised the mended arm and waved him back.

"It's . . . not . . . possible," the doctor stammered.

"What's not?" Scott asked.

The doctor closed the door and cautiously approached the bed. Scott had less difficulty reading the man's thoughts now. He saw terrible confusion, utter dismay. And wonderment as well. But the mind soon reorganized itself, and as the doctor began examining the shoulder, the arm, and the fingers, a clinical exactness masked all hint of feeling.

"All along we've been somewhat confused about your injuries," the doctor confessed. "And there's the matter of your parents. We searched the park for anyone who might know you. We notified the department of human services, the police, even contacted a national hotline for runaways. No one's come forward to identify you in spite of everything."

"I don't live with my parents," Scott explained. "But my uncle must be worried."

17

"I would think so, and yet we haven't heard from him. Maybe you can tell us where we can reach him."

"I don't know," Scott said. "We travel . . . in a mobile home. I don't remember what park he planned to stop at here in Dallas."

"Well, we'll spread the word. I'm certain he'll make himself known. Meanwhile, maybe you could help us. Your name, for instance, place of birth, age, that sort of thing."

"I'm awfully tired," Scott complained.

"But surely these few questions wouldn't strain you too much."

"My name's Scott."

"Yes?" the doctor asked. "Scott what?"

"Scott, uh, Clay," Scott told the man. "I was born in . . . Kansas."

"Date of birth?"

"April 5."

"Well, you mean—"

"It was my birthday, too," Scott acknowledged. "It's why I couldn't let Grant—"

"And your age?"

"Fifteen. Don't suppose I look it, but—"

"Very few people of any age risk their lives to save others, Scott. And appearances, after all, can be very deceiving, can't they? For instance, I would have sworn the fingers of your left hand were crushed past saving. Now they look perfectly normal. Tell me, have you ever had such an accident before? Broken bones, I mean, that seemingly healed themselves?"

"No, sir. I don't believe I've ever been hurt so badly before."

"Would you mind if I had a look at your shoulders? And your back?"

"I guess not," Scott said, searching the doctor's thoughts for an explanation. As he turned over, he finally had an answer. Dr. Edgefield was searching for a birthmark—a clover-shaped splash of brown. He was looking in vain because that mark had been removed years before. But why was this mysterious doctor looking for such a blemish—in the exact spot where it had been?

"Well, that's a shame," the doctor muttered in disappointment.

"Is anything wrong?" Scott asked.

"No, it was the wildest of hunches, after all. Your shoulder appears to have mended perfectly. There aren't even any scars! I stitched a tear in your elbow myself. How are the ribs?"

"Sore," Scott lied.

"Tomorrow I'll remove the bandages and have a look at them. I don't suppose they'll knit as quickly."

"Knit? They don't feel broken."

"I suppose I shouldn't be surprised. Still, your legs will keep you here a few weeks."

"And just where is here?" Scott asked.

"After you've rested a bit more, I'll explain that. It's very complicated. Meanwhile, I understand you had some company. I'll make arrangements for them to return tomorrow. For now, it's best you save your strength. Getting well requires a great deal of energy."

"Yes, it does," Scott confessed with a sly smile.

Once the doctor had departed and the door was closed, Scott busied himself repairing the breaks in his legs. Tendons, muscle, and cartilage had suffered fearfully, and the labor left Scott cold and exhausted.

I was a fool not to wait and do all this back at the ship, he silently told Tiaf. *Now I lack the energy to teleport.*

Only now did Scott notice how naked his fingers appeared. The ring! Where was the ring?

No! What had become of it? Had the convertible crushed the precious emerald along with Scott's fingers? Or did the mysterious doctor have it beneath a microscope? Was it possible so many well-kept secrets might be exposed?

And what of Scott himself? Was he a prisoner in this ivory-white world? What lay ahead? Could anyone believe him ordinary after the mending of fingers and ribs and legs?

What have I done, Tiaf? Scott cried. *Tiaf, old friend, help me!*

But the call brought no answer. What had become of Tiaf, his mentor, his guide, his rescuer?

Scott felt himself drowning in an ocean of uncertainty, beset by questions, and hopelessly lost. He recalled Brian's wrinkled forehead and wondered if his own looked any different.

Where are you, Tiaf? he silently called again. *And what has become of the ring?*

3

Scott found no answers to his questions that long night or the following morning. Often he awoke trembling and confused. Again and again he silently called to Tiaf, but he received no reply.

What's happened to you, old friend? Scott wondered.

He was roused that next morning by a none-too-gentle hand on his shoulder.

"It's time for breakfast," Grant whispered. "How're your legs?"

"Fair," Scott said, trying to flex his knees. The casts wouldn't budge, though, and he felt trapped.

"Not too bad to be moved, are they?" Grant asked.

"No, I'm okay. Why?"

" 'Cause Gigi's swiping a wheelchair. We're going to wheel you down to the cafeteria. You'll never get well eating the slop they feed you here. Down the hall we've got a regular cook."

"Oh?" Scott asked, blinking away his weariness. "You live here, in a hospital?"

21

"Well, it's not a real hospital," Grant said nervously. "Never mind about that for now, though. We better find you some clothes. That thing they put you in hardly covers anything."

"Give me a minute," Scott said, nodding. "I'll find something."

"But—"

"Go look for Gigi," Scott urged. Grant trotted off, and Scott instantly concentrated on the scant hospital gown. He easily transformed it into a pair of shorts, and converted the pillowcase into a T-shirt. By the time Gigi and Grant arrived with the wheelchair, he was sitting on the edge of the bed, ready for his clandestine journey.

"I can't believe you got those shorts on by yourself," Grant whispered as he helped Scott into the wheelchair. "I had a broken leg once, and my mom had to dress me every morning for school. Boy, was that embarrassing!"

"It'll be easier once these casts come off," Scott declared. "I feel like I'm carrying a ball and chain around."

"Yeah, this place has enough of a prison feel," Gigi grumbled. "Classes all the time. Doc or some staff member lurking around, spying on us every minute. Roommates! I envy you, in here by yourself. We never have any time to ourselves."

"Except when we escape," Grant added with a grin. "And school's always seemed like a prison to me. We'd better hurry. Malin's off duty in ten minutes. Then it's the new guy, George."

"We haven't got him trained yet," Gigi explained. "Once these orderlies are here a few weeks, they get to be like family. Till then they take everything too seriously. And George, well, he takes everything Doc says to heart."

22

"And you don't?" Scott asked.

"If we did, we'd never have any fun," Gigi explained. "Don't get me wrong. We take our studies seriously enough. It's just that there are so many stupid rules, like not writing letters or sending postcards, never calling home, keeping to your room during quiet hours. We're kids, not prisoners of war."

Scott was beginning to wonder.

What was clearer was the fact that Gigi and Grant were masters at dodging doctors and orderlies. They took him down one corridor, ducked into an empty closet, hid in a stairwell, and finally spirited him down a second corridor and on to a small dining room. A white-haired woman with a grandmotherly smile was placing platters of sausage and eggs and pancakes on a long serving table.

"Scott, this is Granny Islington," Gigi explained as she wheeled Scott over. "Granny, Scott's staying with us awhile."

"Does Doc know he's down here?" the woman asked.

"More or less," Grant answered.

"Thought so," she said with a scowl. "Well, fill him a plate and steer him to the table. We've food to spare, I suppose. Only I never saw him, hear?"

"It's okay, Granny," one of the twins declared as he led six other young people into the room. "He's a real hero, you know. He saved Grant from getting run over by a car."

"Yeah, Grant would've been squashed flatter than one of your pancakes," the other twin added. The youngsters laughed loudly.

"I suppose you find it funny, looking down on a boy with his legs broken," the woman scolded. "And Grant! Haven't you been warned to keep an eye out for cars?"

She lectured the entire group for a full three minutes, and Scott took note of the fact that not a voice rose to argue. He read the thoughts of the others. Granny, as cook and housekeeper, was no one to anger. He knew, too, the woman possessed a caring, gentle touch. She clearly considered even the oldest among them part of her own private brood.

Once each of the young people had filled a plate, he or she walked to the table and sat down. No one took a bite till the whole group was seated, and only then when Granny nodded to begin. The food itself was delicious, and Scott ate with abandon. Too many days spent surviving on Tiaf's nutrient pills had left Scott hungry for real food. Even when those pills were transformed to look like steak or chicken, the mirages failed to fool Scott's taste buds.

As Gigi swallowed the last bite of her eggs, she began introducing Scott around. She started with a pale-faced, sandy-haired fifteen-year-old named Geoffrey.

"Happy to meet you." Geoff spoke in the accent of his native England. "You play tennis, perhaps?"

"Don't let his size fool you," a tall, blond boy a year older named Jay suggested. "He's a terror on the baselines."

Next came a serious-looking boy named Nathan. Nearly fourteen but small boned and shy, Nathan nevertheless was the only one to offer Scott his hand.

"Hi, Nate," Scott said, gripping the smaller hand firmly. "I'm Scott Clay."

"We don't have last names here," Gigi interrupted. "We're all family."

She then introduced the others. All four were twins. Ivan and Isabella were twelve, yellow haired, and quarrelsome. Isabella was taller by four inches, but it was Ivan who dominated the conversation. His mind was very muddled.

Scott could make no sense of the maze of unrelated thoughts flooding the youngster's skull.

David and Danny, the ten-year-olds, were practically identical in facial features and stature. They might as well have been linked by flesh, for there wasn't anything the one said or did that the other didn't echo. Scott discovered something else, too. Danny and David spoke to each other without words. They were telepathic.

Can you hear me, too? Scott asked silently.

Each twin looked up in turn, confused and nervous. Danny nodded, and David did likewise.

Can you read my thoughts? Scott asked.

Neither could.

It's just as well, Scott thought. He knew he couldn't entirely trust them, though. He would have to guard his thoughts thereafter.

Granny Islington brought in a kettle of hot chocolate and began filling cups. Scott drank his. Then suddenly he felt his chair turn.

"What's the matter?" he asked as Gigi steered him toward the far door. "Is somebody coming?"

You know what's the matter, she answered silently. *We've got to talk!*

Why?

Because you're in my mind, she told him. *And I don't know how or why!*

He nodded, then swallowed the thousands of questions rushing into his head. Such a flood was sure to overwhelm one not well practiced in telepathy. Who could tell what sort of harm Gigi might suffer?

Scott couldn't help grinning as Gigi whirled him out one door, down a narrow ramp, and out some double doors into a small courtyard. There, surrounded by budding roses and bubbling water fountains, she confronted him with her question.

"How?" she demanded.

"If you could hear me, then you understand how," he told her. "You must know you're telepathic. The others, too, I'd guess."

"Not all," she said, frowning. "And not all of us can communicate with one another. I sometimes hear Danny or David. They won't tell Doc, but I think he knows. They do it all the time."

"And you?"

"I can tell Grant things, and sometimes he can answer. We're cousins, you see. I think being related helps, though Doc won't come right out and agree with me."

"What sort of place is this?" Scott asked.

"Don't you know? It's no accident Doc brought you here."

"It's not? I thought it *was* an accident brought me here."

"No, you knew about us at the park. I sensed it. That's why I invited you to stay for lunch."

"I heard your thoughts."

"And Grant's. But you knew more. You had a premonition, didn't you? None of us has ever experienced precognition. But you have."

Scott frowned. He tried to screen his memory from the probing tentacles of her thoughts.

"Don't block me," she pleaded. "Don't you see? I need to know."

"Things aren't always what they appear," he warned. "Trust me to know."

"I'm here, aren't I?" she replied. "Don't you think I know about deceptions myself? We're not in a real school. When we work math problems or read *Treasure Island,* no one seems to care. They only get excited when one of us picks the right shapes from their little decks of cards or predicts the roll of the dice."

"Yeah?" Scott asked. "You mean these doctors and all are really here to study you?"

"And the others. You, too, I suppose."

"That's not possible. How? You've got parents, don't you?"

"I do," she explained. "Grant's folks died in a plane crash. Geoff lost his in a train wreck. Jay's got a mom somewhere, but he never even gets letters. So Doc says, anyway."

"And the twins?"

"The boys were in a foster home. Ivan and Isabella were in a circus. They used to do tricks. Nathan's the only one with a real family. They came to visit once. He misses them."

"Not you?"

"No, I'm sort of a misfit at home. Papa wanted a boy, and he got his wish later on. Three times, in fact. My brothers play ball and go camping—that sort of thing. Mom tried to make up for it by taking me to plays and museums, but I think they were all glad when Doc picked me to come here."

"And what is this place?"

"The Beatrice Romaine Institute," Gigi explained. "Some rich old lady left a bunch of money so her dead spirit could talk to the living. Anyway, Doc's taken over."

"And he studies telepathy."

"Oh, more than that. The staff runs rats through mazes, does all sorts of experiments. Sometimes Doc lets us watch.

They're working on some sort of communications equipment, too."

"And what's that got to do with you?"

"We're an experiment of sorts too. We all have E.S.P. When I first came here we played guessing games. You know, tell what object they're hiding behind a screen. Nobody had much real luck at that. Forty percent was my tops. Then came the implants. Now we practice mental exercises. In time he expects us to quadruple our power."

"Just what are these implants, Gigi?" Scott asked as he felt a wave of pain sweep through her mind.

"I don't altogether understand it. I could draw you pictures, though. Doc came up with the idea that the reason human beings have such limited psi powers is that our minds aren't able to focus. So he planted small electrodes in our brains. They form a sort of electronic amplifier, boosting our thoughts."

"You mean—"

"Yes, I let him cut me open and put a microchip in my head!" she exclaimed, parting her hair so he could detect the tiny scar. "The others too. Wouldn't you if somebody told you you'd be able to move objects around a table, read minds, maybe even teleport? Imagine moving yourself from place to place by sheer will!"

"And your parents agreed to all this?"

"Mine did. I don't know everything, but Dad mentioned they were getting money. And we're getting paid, too."

"It can't be just money."

"It's not," she confessed. "Scott, we're misfits, all nine of us. There's not a one of us, except maybe Nathan, who's wanted at home, and even he'd tell you he didn't fit in there or at school. Doc says we could well be skipping a step on the evolutionary ladder. We could be the first new humans."

Scott scowled and turned his chair back toward the door.

"I thought for certain you'd understand," she grumbled. "He brought you here, too, didn't he? Didn't he promise you anything?"

"No," Scott said. "We've hardly talked. He can't keep me here. I won't stay."

"Where will you go? Your uncle hasn't come."

"He wouldn't. He's sort of a recluse. I'll go to him."

"You mean that, don't you? You aren't staying."

"Read the truth of it in my thoughts," he told her.

"Scott, I see it there. So much more, too. I thought you were one of us, but you're not. You know so much more than you'll allow me to see. I'm scared. Why did I tell you all this?"

"Because we're alike," he said, turning back to face her.

"Alike? How?"

"Different. It's awfully hard to be different, isn't it, Gigi? People laugh at you. They make up jokes. And you can never really share everything, not even with your friends."

"No," she said, rubbing a tear from her eye. "Not with your mom or brothers or anybody."

"Still, it doesn't mean some doctor has a right to make experiments out of you. To treat you like guinea pigs."

"We came here of our own choice," she declared. "And at least here we're not alone."

"No?" Scott asked, feeling lonelier than ever before in his life. "What about me? Did I have any choice?"

"I don't know," she confessed.

"Gigi, tell me something else. When I came here, I wore a ring."

29

"I remember it," she said, rising to her feet. "It was beautiful. Bright green with some strange characters across the base."

"Did you see it after the car hit me? Was it damaged when my fingers were crushed?"

"They *were* crushed, weren't they? You fixed them! Show me how, won't you? I want to be a doctor when I'm older."

"What about the ring, Gigi?" Scott demanded.

"Doc took it. It's probably in his office."

"Can you sneak me in there? You seem able to get everywhere else."

"Not in there," she said, shuddering. "Doc's got a friendly face, Scott, but you wouldn't want to cross him. I read him sometimes. He's done some horrible things."

"Then just tell me where his office is," Scott pleaded.

"Not me," she said, gripping the chair and wheeling it back toward the corridor. "I've said too much already!"

4

Grant met them halfway down the hall and took charge of Scott's wheelchair.

"Doc's been asking about you, Gigi," the boy explained. "Mrs. Wallace's been looking for the wheelchair, and George said he saw you with it."

"Leave it to George to tell him," Gigi growled. "See if you can sneak it back, will you, Grant?"

"I'm good at that," Grant said, grinning. "Come on, Scott, I'll get you back to your room first."

Scott nodded, and Grant soon had the chair zooming down one corridor and back up another. They ducked into only one closet, and that was to avoid the tall, stone-faced orderly named George. Once back in the room Scott climbed into his bed, and Grant hurried off to return the wheelchair.

Alone, Scott tried to make some sense of his predicament. There he was, stranded in a mysterious institute! Why? Who was Dr. Edgefield, anyway? And why couldn't he reach Tiaf?

"Well, one thing's certain," Scott grumbled as he stared

at his encased legs. "I'm going nowhere with these casts on my legs!"

Freeing oneself from several pounds of plaster was no simple task. Scott was angry, though, and he concentrated his rage on those casts. He felt the plaster growing warm as he focused his energy. Then a seam suddenly burst open, and the casts split apart as if torn by a giant invisible can opener.

"There," Scott said, kicking his legs free. He was pretty well covered with a crusty sort of powder, but it didn't matter. He'd regained his liberty.

If only I had my ring, Scott thought. But he didn't.

Scott lay on the bed, flexing his knees and feeling the blood revive his tortured muscles. Again he unsuccessfully tried to contact Tiaf. Scott felt alone, isolated. What was it about this place that chilled him so?

He knew he had to escape, but how? What would the doctors say if he started down those corridors on his own? But then they surely had questions enough already.

He hopped off the bed and took a step toward the door, but at that same moment it moved toward him. Scott froze. He expected Dr. Edgefield, or perhaps the tall orderly, George. Instead Grant stepped inside.

"What happened?" the boy asked, gazing at the discarded casts. "Doc do that?"

"No, I did," Scott explained. "I didn't need them."

"Didn't . . ."

"My legs are fine," Scott said, bending his knees and making a turn. "See?"

"I don't see how a guy can get hit by a car and not get something broken!" Grant exclaimed.

"I'm pretty quick on my feet."

"You're a fast runner, I'll say that. You raced across the park like nothing I ever saw before. Still . . ."

"You know where Dr. Edgefield's office is, Grant?" Scott asked.

"I know," the boy admitted. "Nobody goes there, though."

"You're pretty clever. Figure you can get me in there?"

"No way, Scott. It's always locked. I think it's where they keep the drugs and stuff. What do you want there?"

"I had a ring. I think the doctor might have it there."

"If he does, you'll never see it. Why don't you ask him about it?"

"I wouldn't want him to think it was . . . valuable."

"Yeah, he'd keep it for sure then. Hey, can you walk?"

"Sure," Scott said.

"We're leaving in about an hour on a field trip to the art museum. Want to come?"

"I don't imagine I'm invited."

"Hey, Malin's driving us," Grant said, grinning. "He never asks questions. I'll bet Geoff's got some clothes you can borrow. You two are about the same size. Guess maybe you could use a shower, too. That plaster makes a mess, doesn't it?"

"Sure does," Scott agreed.

Grant then led Scott outside and down the corridor. Once again they played a game of hide and seek with the various doctors, technicians, and orderlies. Scott reached a large community shower room unspotted, though, and Grant nudged him inside.

"There are towels in the cabinet," the boy explained. "I'll be back in a bit with some clothes."

"Don't forget shoes," Scott called.

"Size?"

"Seven and a half."

"Got it," Grant said, waving farewell. "Be back in a flash."

Actually, though, Scott had showered and nearly finished drying off when Grant returned. The English boy, Geoff, arrived a moment later carrying a stack of clothes. Grant brought the shoes himself.

"They're eights," Grant explained as he set them alongside the bench where Scott sat drying his hair. "Some Jay outgrew. Hope they're close."

"I expect these will fit better," Geoff added as he presented the clothes. "Welcome to them, and to my place in the van as well. I have no stomach for old tombs."

"It's an Egyptian exhibit we're seeing," Grant explained. "Not everybody's going, so there's plenty of room in the van."

"Won't anybody notice it's me and not Geoff?" Scott asked.

"Malin might notice," Geoff said, laughing. "But he wouldn't say anything."

"Malin's got a motto," Grant added. "As long as we don't bring him trouble, he keeps things to himself."

"Griselda's gone to make up your bed," Geoff remarked. "So Doc's sure to think you're resting."

"Griselda?" Scott asked.

"Gigi," Grant explained. "I'd change my name, too, if it was that bad. Better hurry now. We leave soon."

Scott nodded and accelerated his pace. In a matter of minutes he was dry, dressed, and ready.

"I still don't understand about your legs," Grant said,

staring at Scott's bare calves. "I saw them. There was lots of blood, and one bone was sticking through the skin!"

"You were probably excited," Scott argued.

"Maybe, but there's not even a scar."

"I heal well."

"Fast, too," Grant said, gazing at Scott suspiciously.

"Likely he thinks you're an android," Geoff suggested. "He's built himself a robot, you see."

"Doc locked it up," Grant explained.

"After it short-circuited the hall relays," Geoff added with a laugh. "But there's time for such talk later, and tennis as well. You two had best hurry to the van."

Grant nodded, and Scott started to collect his discarded hospital gown.

"I'll tend to that," Geoff insisted. "Now get along."

Scott left eagerly. Grant continued to play his game of dodge the orderlies, but once outside, the boy seemed to undergo a transformation. Gigi waved them aboard, and they took the three backseats, leaving the two pairs of twins the center benches. Nathan sat up front.

"Everybody aboard?" a youngish-looking man with shaggy brown hair and a wide smile called as he climbed into the driver's seat.

"All that's going, Malin," Ivan announced.

"Then we're outa here," the driver said, starting the engine. In no time the van was roaring down a long concrete driveway and onto a busy Dallas street. As Malin drove, he struck up old country songs. His voice was more whine than melody, but David and Danny joined in.

"Kids," Grant grumbled.

"Cheer up," Gigi urged. "We'll soon be climbing around

on mummies and deciphering hieroglyphics. He wants to be an archaeologist, you know."

"I didn't," Scott confessed.

"That or study avionics," Grant explained. "I haven't really decided."

"You've got a day or so left," Scott pointed out. "Did you get into trouble about the wheelchair, Gigi?"

"Funny thing," she said, laughing. "It turned out to be right where it was supposed to be. No, Doc just griped at George and Mrs. Wallace for bothering him."

"What did he say to you?" Scott asked, reading something unspoken in her eyes.

"He suggested she should concentrate on her studies," Grant said, frowning. "That's right, isn't it? I can read you pretty well away from the Institute, Gigi."

"That's right," she admitted. "Grant, Scott can read me, too. And he's had no implant."

"What?" the boy asked. He hastily examined Scott's scalp. "Okay, tell me what I'm thinking," Grant demanded.

Scott concentrated. He read a jumble of thoughts, and it was difficult to unscramble them. Finally he detected one common thread. Grant was recalling the scantily clad cyclists from the lakeside park.

"Well, I don't quite know how to put this," Scott said, grinning. "It has to do with bicycles, though, and—"

"That's enough," Grant said, blushing. "You're right, Gigi. He can read my thoughts. He's telepathic."

"He knew about the speeding car, too," she added. "He saw it happen."

"You're precognitive?" Grant asked.

"Shhh," Scott pleaded. "You don't have to tell the whole world. It's going to be hard enough getting away."

36

"Doc doesn't know yet," Gigi observed. "Once he does, he'll find a way to make sure you stay."

"You don't understand," Scott objected. "I've got my uncle. And a place to go."

"You'd better make a break for it at the museum," Grant suggested. "Otherwise Doc'll find out. He always does. And then you'll have somebody watching you all the time."

"He's right," Gigi agreed. "Maybe you should call your uncle and get him to come for you."

"Maybe," Scott admitted. But he had no intention of leaving without the ring. In truth, he wasn't sure he could without it.

They reached the Dallas Museum of Art in half an hour. It wasn't at all what Scott had expected. Most museums he'd visited resembled old marble or granite tombs. This place was modern and full of light. Outside, modern sculptures defied description. Inside, a huge Egyptian statue of primitive stone marked the special exhibit.

"It's Ramesses II," Scott muttered as he stepped closer. "I remember."

"Oh, you've been here before," Grant grumbled.

"No," Scott said, standing in silent awe beside the towering statue.

"The exhibit's been on tour," Nathan explained, joining the discussion. "So, did you see it in Boston, or maybe in Charlotte? My aunt wrote me from Raleigh that she'd seen Ramesses. She called the displays outstanding."

"No, not in Charlotte," Scott said as he read the cryptic legend on the base.

"Okay, guys, over here," Malin called then, holding up a handful of tickets. "Now behave yourselves. Don't want Doc hearing you caused trouble."

37

"No, Malin," they all agreed.

The orderly handed them their tickets, then explained how he'd return with the van in two hours.

"We'll have ourselves a late lunch and then go back," Malin concluded. "Gigi, you're in charge. Keep an eye on Ivan and see he doesn't steal any mummies."

"I wouldn't," Ivan insisted.

"You'd swipe King Tut's beard if it was handy," Isabella countered. "You set off any alarms, Ivan, and we'll hang you by your toes out the window."

"Can't," Ivan said, grinning. "You'd set off the burglar alarms."

"We'll do something," Nathan threatened. "And that would be in addition to any ancient curses the Egyptians might have cast on the defiler of Ramesses the Great."

Ivan shrank from those words, and Nathan immediately began spinning a tale of cursed grave diggers and the like. Scott, meanwhile, drifted past the big statue to where several panels of hieroglyphics stood inviting inspection.

"These have never been completely translated," a museum guide explained. "These small figures refer to Ramesses, though, by some of his many names."

"Yes, I see them," Scott replied, pointing to the panels in question. "Mostly this panel tells of the pharoah's great victory at Kadesh. See here? This indicates the great Hittite host that was set upon."

The guide nodded, then made an awkward escape.

"You know all that?" Grant asked. "I've studied up and I can't make out more than a few glyphs."

"It's just a kind of symbolic writing," Scott explained. As he began to translate some of the figures, Gigi grew pale.

"That isn't possible," she blurted out.

"What?" Scott asked.

"You can't have been there."

"Of course not," Scott said, shuddering as he realized she was scanning his mind.

"Luxor. You're remembering Luxor," she cried.

"Just a book I read about it," Scott insisted. "I'd be thousands of years old if I'd lived back then."

"Sure—he read about it," Grant said, laughing uneasily.

The guide returned and urged both silence and respect. Scott moved along to another display, but Gigi pursued him.

"I know what I read," she declared.

"You've read a lot of minds, have you? Well, did it occur to you maybe my imagination was hard at work, imagining the temples, creating a daydream?"

"Complete with the words of a scribe interpreting the glyphs?" she asked, unconvinced. "I don't know how, Scott, but I know what I sense to be the truth."

"It might be better if you didn't," he declared.

They spent the remainder of the time at the museum exploring the artifacts. Scott translated other panels, but he took care to mask his mind from his companions. He himself could hear their thoughts as clearly as if they were spoken. And for the first time he realized how readily Grant and Gigi communicated.

Malin appeared right on schedule, picked up the students, and drove to a nearby pizza parlor. After stuffing themselves with pizza and ice cream, the younger ones assaulted a video arcade. Gigi, Grant and Nathan devoted themselves to a mind-reading game.

"Join us," Grant urged. "It's a rare chance to swap gossip and not get in trouble. At the Institute somebody's always listening in. And reception's terrible."

"Well, what do you expect with all that electronic garbage Doc's set up," Nathan complained.

You mean you can't read each other as easily there? Scott silently asked his companions. Each of them answered with a strong yes. He nodded his own understanding, then set off for the rest room. Once safely in the corner stall, Scott called out to Tiaf.

Where are you, young friend? Tiaf's voice replied. *Are you well? Hurt?*

I'm well, Tiaf, Scott answered.

Return immediately. I sense terrible peril.

I know, Scott admitted. He sensed rare fear in Tiaf's thoughts. Now that the door was open to escape, though, his own thoughts drifted back to the Institute.

Return, Scott, Tiaf pleaded.

I don't have my ring, Scott explained. *There are things I need to discover, too.*

Come back, Tiaf urged.

Soon, Scott promised. *When I retrieve my ring.*

Tiaf's pleas continued to echo through Scott's mind. Then they stopped.

Yes, I hear them, the old man communicated. *These others are not like us. Children mutilated! Scott, there is terrible danger.*

He knew. But he also worried about the dangers facing his new friends. And there was Dr. Edgefield. What if he discovered the power of that ring? Or if he guessed Scott's secret?

5

When the Institute van pulled up into the driveway, it was met by a trio of doctors in white lab coats. Dr. Victor Edgefield was in the center, hands crossed across his stomach.

"Somebody's in for it," Ivan declared. "Doc's mad."

That proved to be an understatement. The doctor threw open the door and ordered the passengers marched off to their rooms.

"Dr. Thomas," Dr. Edgefield added, "see to it personally. Dr. Faulkner, take charge of our guest."

Dr. Faulkner gripped Scott's hand securely as he stepped out of the van. Dr. Edgefield then started in on Malin.

"Come along," Dr. Faulkner told Scott. "That's none of your business."

"Isn't he in trouble for taking me along?" Scott asked her. "For letting me escape your clutches for a few hours?"

"He's in trouble for disobeying Institute policy," she answered.

"And what am I in trouble for?" Scott asked as he shook loose of her grip.

"You aren't in trouble," she insisted. "We were merely worried about you. You've had a severe shock and considerable trauma."

"I'm fine," Scott argued.

"We'll be in a better position to discuss that when we conclude our examination," she told him. "Come along now. We have preparations to make."

It didn't seem reasonable to argue just then. After all, Dr. Faulkner wasn't making any decisions. In the end Scott knew it was Dr. Edgefield who would call the tune. Scott would save his words for him.

"It was wrong for you to leave without telling anybody," Dr. Faulkner said as they approached the hospital wing of the Institute. "Very wrong. You had us all concerned."

"Concerned?" Scott asked. "How do you think my uncle's been feeling?"

"You spoke with him?"

"I did. He would've come after me at the museum, except Dr. Edgefield took some of my things. I want them back."

"What things?" Dr. Edgefield asked, joining them at the door of the sterile white room. He wore a heavy frown.

"My clothes," Scott barked. "And my ring!"

"Lower your voice, young man," the man commanded. "First of all, your clothes were little more than bloody rags. We cut the shirt away to treat your ribs, and the shorts weren't much to begin with."

"My shoes," Scott growled.

"I have no idea what's become of them, but you're welcome to what you're wearing. Jay confessed to giving

42

them to you. He and Geoff are being punished, by the way. As Griselda and Grant will be."

"And my ring? I suppose you conveniently lost that."

"It's in my safe," Dr. Edgefield explained. "The stone's an actual emerald. Did you know that?"

"I did."

"Seems strange that a boy your age should have such a valuable piece of jewelry. The police are checking to make certain it isn't stolen."

"It's not."

"We have only your word on that, Scott, and I fear your word hasn't proven very reliable. For instance, I can't seem to find evidence of any Scott Clay having been born in Kansas on the date you provided."

"Well, I wasn't any too conscious at the time. Maybe it wasn't Kansas. Maybe it was a day before or after. Maybe you didn't check all the courthouses."

"And maybe you're lying to me," Dr. Edgefield complained as he nudged Scott inside his room before shutting the door. Dr. Edgefield led Dr. Faulkner inside a moment afterward. Dr. Thomas arrived a bit later.

"Just what in heaven's name are you doing?" Dr. Edgefield asked as he pointed to the remains of the discarded casts resting beside the bed. "Did you think we wouldn't find that? Did you think no one would notice you walking around on a pair of broken legs?"

"They're not broken," Scott argued. "Look for yourself. See any breaks?"

"And these?" Dr. Thomas asked, holding up a sheet of X-ray film. "I took them myself. I counted three compound and two simple fractures. Your legs are a jigsaw puzzle, young man."

"Are they?" Scott asked, hopping onto the bed and dangling his legs before the physicians. "What do you see?"

"X rays don't lie," Dr. Faulkner declared.

"Maybe somebody mixed up the plates. I don't know. But my legs are just fine, and I didn't see any reason to wear those stupid casts."

The doctors exchanged glances. Dr. Faulkner knelt beside the bed and made a brief examination. Dr. Thomas gazed at the X rays and shook his head. Confusion reigned in his eyes. As for Dr. Edgefield, he was equally and utterly mystified. Scott couldn't resist grinning.

"We've still had no word from your parents, Scott," Dr. Edgefield said, scowling.

"My uncle, you mean," Scott pointed out.

"Oh, yes, your uncle."

"I have. I spoke with him from the pizza place. He wanted me to leave right then, but as I said, there's the ring. It was my father's, you see, and I want it back."

"In time, Scott," Edgefield said. "Once the police finish checking. And after we have a look at it. Those strange markings—they're quite old, I suspect. Not Greek. Phoenician perhaps."

"I don't know," Scott answered evasively. "I just know it's mine. I want it back. And I want to leave!"

"Scott, surely you understand we can't simply release you," Dr. Faulkner told him. "Not on your own. There are papers to sign, legal questions to address. Perhaps you'd give me your uncle's phone number. I could contact him for you."

"Maybe he could come here and pick you up," Dr. Edgefield suggested.

"He hasn't got much use for hospitals," Scott replied.

44

"Nor for doctors. You keep me much longer, though, and I'll bet he gets to know a couple of lawyers."

The threat brought a nervous tremor to Dr. Thomas, and Dr. Faulkner gave Dr. Edgefield a concerned glance.

"We have a special relationship with federal and local authorities," he explained. "But all this talk is producing nothing. I'm certain Scott is weary from his explorations. Let's give him some time to think, shall we? Later we'll speak more."

The other doctors nodded their agreement, and they left immediately. Scott half believed himself triumphant. But when he tried to call Tiaf, there was no reply. Upon opening the door, Scott found the tall orderly, George, posted outside.

"Get back into that bed, boy," George barked. "You got me in enough trouble today, you and them wheelchair-stealin' brat friends o' yours."

Scott started to object, but George pushed him inside and closed the door. Scott remained in the room all evening, more alone than he'd imagined possible. George brought a food tray at six o'clock. Otherwise no one moved in or out of the door. It was as if the gates of the dungeon had been slammed shut.

As for the night, it proved anything but restful. Time after time Scott was besieged by the thoughts of others. First George and then another orderly embarked on fantasy holidays. A technician worried over her sick baby and resented the efforts expended on behalf of the Institute's spoiled darlings. And from time to time Scott picked up thoughts from the other children. Mostly those minds were a disorganized jumble, though, and Scott was powerless to channel clear messages through the maze of extra matter.

Tiaf, help me make sense of it, Scott pleaded. *Where are you? Why can't your mind reach me?*

Scott slept in spurts. Often, as he floated peacefully in a dream world, thoughts would strike like lightning bolts and bring him to consciousness.

"The ring is only an amplifier," Tiaf had once said. Scott recalled that vividly. "In time you won't need it."

Maybe I don't need it now, Scott thought. *Maybe I can free myself from this prison by teleporting away, ring or no ring.*

He tried. He concentrated until his head throbbed. Sweat rolled off his forehead and stung his eyes. He thought once his skull might simply explode. But he went nowhere. Simple tasks like moving objects or crafting images remained possible. But something seemed to block his mind, sap his strength, hold him in that room.

Scott turned in frustration to his window. He concentrated on the thick pane and heavy steel frame. He hoped to melt each in turn. As he worked, the aching in his head increased. He could feel a terrific heat disturb the molecular composition of the steel. Ions sped violently. Mentally Scott fought to transform the pane, but he was too weak. His head pounded. Outside, in the corridor, feet scurried about. Voices shouted, and Scott heard the low hum of machinery.

"It's not possible, Doc!" a voice cried. "Look at where the readings register. Not beta or theta waves!"

"This is it!" Dr. Edgefield proclaimed. "Zeta transmissions. We've broken through!"

Scott felt a sudden shudder as people rushed down the corridor again. Now came a new sound, a deep melodic drumming that swept first one direction, then another.

"Oh, no," Scott muttered. "It's a directional finder."

Instantly he wiped his mind clear, but it was too late. The three doctors rushed past George and dashed into the room.

"I tell you it's not possible," Dr. Thomas argued. "Vic, he isn't even one of the sample group. He hasn't had the surgery!"

"Maybe he doesn't need it," Dr. Edgefield argued. "Scott, are you still awake? You are, aren't you?"

"If I answer, can I leave?" Scott asked.

"Soon," the chief doctor declared. "First we need to run some tests."

"Tests?" Scott cried. "Don't I have any sayso over that?"

"No," Dr. Thomas replied.

"Then I'm a prisoner here," Scott announced.

"Naturally not," Dr. Edgefield objected. "Our guest. Honored guest, in point of fact. I have a feeling that we almost met before. If we had, you would certainly have been invited to the Institute."

"And if I turned down that invitation?" Scott asked.

Dr. Edgefield didn't answer. He smiled and offered compliments, but there was something unspoken in his mind.

He's not telling all, Scott realized. *His is a disciplined mind, accustomed to subterfuge. And not easily fooled.*

The doctors allowed him an uneasy rest. That next morning, though, they wheeled him to an examination room. Once there, they placed him on a flat cart and strapped his arms and legs down. His head was secured next.

"Relax, Scott," Dr. Faulkner urged as she patted his clenched fist. "We're not going to hurt you. It's a simple procedure. You won't be harmed."

He didn't answer. He could read their suspicions, the myriad questions floating through their heads. Scott felt helpless. He was a laboratory specimen undergoing examination. Nothing more.

They began by taking X rays. Scott did his best to squirm, hoping to blur the pictures. The restraints were tight, though, and he could do little more than move his fingers and toes. Next they tapped and probed every inch of him. Skin scrapings were put under a microscope. They took so many blood samples that Scott began to feel like a pincushion.

Dr. Thomas supervised a painful spinal tap. Then Dr. Faulkner performed a brain scan.

"There's nothing out of the ordinary," Dr. Faulkner announced as Scott stared angrily up at her.

"No pain?" he whispered. "No harm?"

"We have to find out," she said, avoiding the betrayal etched into his face. "We're almost finished now."

She rested a hand on his chest and waited for his heartbeat to slow. Then Dr. Thomas placed electrodes on his chest and forehead. They ran their impulses through him. The current stung his senses, brought fresh flashes of pain.

"Stop it!" Dr. Faulkner ordered. "Can't you see it's hurting him?"

For a moment Scott thought his brain would explode. Then, shuddering, he unleashed a furious silent scream. Needles on instruments jumped, and electrodes shorted out. Tubes popped and circuits fused. The straps holding his arms in place shredded.

"My God!" Dr. Faulkner cried as she leaped away from the cart. "Shut off the equipment!"

Scott stared hatefully at his persecutors. Then he closed

his eyes and masked his mind. Instantly dials and meters dropped.

"What's happened?" Dr. Thomas shouted in alarm.

"He's turned himself off," Dr. Edgefield explained.

"That's not possible," Dr. Thomas argued. "There's no measurable brain activity at all! It's just not possible to switch off the brain."

"Not for us," Dr. Edgefield admitted. "But for him . . ."

They went on debating Scott's state, discussing the strange results of their tests. Scott tuned them out. Nothing really mattered. He'd revealed too much of himself to them. Now they would never let him go. There would be tests and more tests, questions he wouldn't answer, a universe of pain and torment.

Tiaf? Scott called again and again. He received no answer.

Finally a pair of orderlies wheeled Scott back to his room. Another brought a breakfast tray. The guard remained outside, though, and Scott soured. He wouldn't touch the food, and when the three doctors visited, he closed his eyes and ignored them.

"You can't avoid us forever," Dr. Edgefield complained.

Scott only stared blankly at the window.

Dr. Faulkner took the food tray outside, and the other doctors followed. For several minutes they argued loudly.

"He's got to eat, Victor!" Dr. Faulkner finally exclaimed. "You were wrong to order all those tests done today. He needs time to adjust!"

"I need answers!" Dr. Edgefield insisted.

"You won't get them this way," she complained.

The hall froze in silence a moment or two. Then Dr. Faulkner stepped back inside, minus the tray.

"Cheer up, Scott," she said, smiling. "I know you're confused and feeling hurt, but this isn't such a bad place. Give us a chance."

Sure, he thought. What choice do I have?

Maybe it was fear that convinced Dr. Edgefield to permit Gigi and Grant to visit. Or perhaps they wormed their way past the orderlies. Scott didn't know. He only saw in their pale faces a crack in the wall of isolation that held him captive.

"What have they done to you?" Gigi asked, touching Scott lightly on the shoulder. "You look terrible."

"Better eat something," Grant suggested.

Scott couldn't help grinning when Grant dumped half a dozen candy bars onto his bed.

"Just ran some tests," Scott explained as he unwrapped a Zero bar.

"Yeah, I remember," Gigi said, nodding. "That's how it was when we first got here. You get so tired of being pricked and scanned, and well, I wanted to scream. Doc says you refuse to eat, though. You're not sick, are you?"

"Just sick of him," Scott answered as he bit into the candy.

"He doesn't trust the food," Grant said. "It's not great, but we've never been drugged or poisoned. Doc said to tell you he's sorry the tests hurt you."

"I'll just bet," Scott grumbled.

"It's all my fault," Grant lamented as he sat on the bed beside Scott. "If I would've been more careful and if you hadn't gotten in the way of that car—"

"Hey, it's okay," Scott said, elbowing Grant's ribs lightly. "Nobody's died. I sure wish I'd taken off yesterday morning, though."

50

"I'm glad you didn't," Gigi said.

"Gigi, what do you do here?" Scott asked.

"Research," she explained. "Parapsychic research. I told you about it earlier."

"Just E.S.P. at first," Grant added. "Then other stuff. They expect us to become telepathic."

"We practice telekinesis, too," Gigi explained, "but even amplified, we can't manage much beyond rolling a toy car across a table."

"Doc says it's just the beginning, though," Grant added. "He says in time we'll be able to open and close doors, maybe even teleport—move without vehicles."

"What makes him think so?" Scott asked.

"I'm not certain," Gigi confessed. "Once when I was with Doc in the lab, he was studying some reports. I read his thoughts. We aren't the first kids he's worked with. There was a boy who could do all sorts of things. I've always thought it funny that Doc isn't interested in what we can do. We're not being studied. We're being taught."

"Developed," Grant said, frowning. "Changed."

"But changed into what?" Gigi asked.

Scott suspected he knew, but he masked his thoughts from his friends. They, after all, had troubles enough.

"Gigi," Scott said, swallowing hard, "you said at the museum that you receive better away from the Institute. Why's that?"

"Well," she said, exchanging a nervous look with Grant, "Doc's got monitors and equipment all over this place. It causes electronic interference."

"Yeah?" he asked, probing for something more, something unspoken and now hidden from him.

"Please," Gigi cried, clasping her hands to her head. "I can't tell you. You're hurting me!"

Scott turned away and slammed his fist against the bed.

"You're a prisoner here too," Scott declared. "Don't hide things from me. I have to know. For all our sakes."

"For your sake," she replied. "I'm not so sure about the rest of us."

"You don't trust me?" Scott asked.

"You don't trust us," she countered. "How much have you shared, Scott? How did you mend your broken bones? How did you get rid of those casts?"

"You're right," Scott confessed. "I haven't shared it all. You wouldn't like what I would tell you, though. I know."

"Maybe you wouldn't like what I'd say, either," she countered. "And it wouldn't make any difference. There's no escaping the Institute. Not for any of us."

"She's right," Grant said, passing Scott another candy bar. "We better go now, Scott. I'm sorry we got you into this."

"You didn't," Scott told them. "It's my nature to jump in where any fool would stay clear. It's gotten me in trouble before."

He read their thoughts then. They warned he'd never known real trouble before. It lay just ahead.

"Thanks for the food," Scott said as his visitors turned to leave. "The talk, too. I was starved for both."

"We'll come again," Grant promised. "When we can."

"Good," Scott told them. "I look forward to it."

Gigi paused, then stepped over and clasped his hands.

"Be careful," she urged. "And patient."

Scott nodded, but he determined to be neither. After they left he lay on his bed and concentrated every fiber of his being. He imagined the ship, saw Tiaf at its controls. He fixed it in his mind and fought to transport himself there. Without the ring, though, he lacked the ability to focus. And his head began to throb as never before.

Tiaf? he called. *Oh, Tiaf, why can't I hear you? I'm so alone, so lost. Bring me home, won't you?*

No answer came. No comforting hands worked the agony from his temples or calmed his trembling shoulders.

Scott had never been so hopelessly alone!

6

He remained in isolation the balance of the day and all night. Then, the following morning, without explanation George roused him before breakfast, presented him with a stack of clean clothes, and directed him to the shower room.

"You've been reassigned," the orderly told Scott. "Room Twelve. It's down the corridor on the right."

"Why?" Scott asked.

"Doc says you've been admitted to the Institute. That's all I know, kid. I guess he'll tell you anything he wants you to know."

Scott probed the tall man's thoughts. Nothing was hidden. It was as George said, or as he had been told at any rate. Scott didn't argue. As he stepped through the shower-room doorway, Grant offered a welcoming hand, and Ivan immediately dumped a pail of water over Scott's startled head.

"Should've expected that, I suppose," Scott said, shaking his head. "You managed to get my clothes all wet, Ivan. Dr. Edgefield won't be any too happy about that."

"You won't tell him, will you?" Ivan said, growing pale.

"I know where the clothes dryer is. Give me ten minutes. I'll have them ready for you."

"It's not fair Ivan should get into trouble," Jay declared. "We were all in on it."

The others nodded, and Scott passed the clothes over to Ivan. The boy rushed out the door.

"Ivan and the twins are pretty scared of Doc," Grant explained. "They're special, being twins. He works them harder."

"Works?" Scott asked.

"You'll see," Nathan grumbled. "He'll have you playing his games too."

Scott showered hurriedly. He was still drying himself when Ivan reappeared with the dry clothes. Scott nodded his thanks and began dressing.

"I see what Grant meant," Jay commented as he gazed intently at Scott's left hand. "I saw those fingers myself. They were crushed by a wheel!"

"No, I pulled away in time," Scott insisted.

Did you? David asked, sitting on the far end of the bench and staring intently. *I can hear you, Scott. How?*

Scott hadn't paid much attention to the others. He had his own worries, after all. Now, though, as Danny and David came close, Scott noticed a small reddish-brown blemish on each twin's left shoulder.

Doc noticed that, too, Danny explained.

He was disappointed it wasn't clover-shaped, David added.

Then Scott read something half hidden by the twins. Their father had had a like birthmark, only it *was* shaped like a clover.

"You know why, don't you?" Danny asked.

We'll speak of it elsewhere, Scott told them. *Whatever you do, don't tell Dr. Edgefield. You could be in danger.*

Danger? David asked.

Scott nodded subtly, and the twins moved back to the far end of the bench.

"You were talking with them, weren't you?" Grant asked.

"Not exactly talking," Scott declared.

"Reading them then. Inside the Institute. I've never been able to do that with anybody but Gigi, and only with her now and then. But I hear you when you want me to. And I can read you if you let me."

"It's all a matter of concentration," Scott said as he slid a T-shirt over his bony shoulders. "Let's get to breakfast, okay?"

"Sure," Grant muttered.

Scott enjoyed the delights of Granny Islington's table. Except for the chocolate bars Grant had brought, Scott had gone without food for most of a day. He hadn't trusted the trays George had brought. Now, though, with the others sharing the same platters of eggs and bacon, Scott ate till he was stuffed.

Scott found himself the subject of questioning eyes as he scanned the length of the table. The others weren't entirely at ease. He listened to their suspicions, read their concerns. It was only natural, after all, to wonder about miraculously cured bones and precognitions of tragedy.

Scott made no effort to answer them. He wasn't ready to share his secrets. Not then, anyway, and probably not ever.

Scott himself was more than a little curious about what Dr. Edgefield occupied his charges with. The Institute devoted only two hours each day to textbook study.

"Is this all?" Scott asked Gigi when Dr. Faulkner conducted them to a series of small cubicles.

"We're pretty advanced," she explained. "Even Ivan reads at college level. Why waste time working math problems when you can do advanced analysis? Doc says he could get any one of us into college tomorrow."

"So what *do* you do?"

"Listen and find out," Dr. Faulkner suggested as she pointed Gigi toward one cubicle and steered Scott to another. Soon they were each assigned varying mental exercises.

Scott sat at his assigned chair and stared at a blank wall in front of him.

"Here, Scott," Dr. Faulkner said, placing a set of earphones on his head. He listened to strange, distorted sounds and tried to make some sense of them. Others did the same. Suddenly the noises clarified, and Scott grew cold. A voice was giving landing coordinates. Another spoke of meteor damage.

"Can you make any sense of it?" Dr. Faulkner asked.

"Who made these noises?" Scott asked. "Whales?"

"Maybe no one," the doctor answered. "Most of them are random radio waves. But they all bear striking similarity in frequency and length to certain communications we have monitored here at the Institute."

"Telepathy, you mean."

"You know about that, do you? Well, Dr. Edgefield suspects some of these sounds may actually be space communications."

"By aliens, no doubt," Scott suggested, attempting to laugh it all off.

"Don't be so quick to discount it," she advised. "We've had a degree of proof that visitors have come to Earth."

"Yeah, they built the pyramids, didn't they?"

"Maybe. We've had the opportunity to study certain individuals as well. Mostly we only find more questions, but Dr. Edgefield expects in time we'll learn more."

"Does he?" Scott asked. "Well, it's interesting to consider."

"Haven't you ever wondered if perhaps there aren't other civilizations out there, Scott?"

"Me? I can't even get out of this place and back to my uncle. What do I care if Martians are landing in New Jersey?"

"Oh, I don't think we've found any evidence there. But in New Mexico—"

Dr. Faulkner was cut short by Dr. Edgefield's arrival. He motioned for Scott to discard his headphones and follow. Scott did so only after satisfying himself that Dr. Edgefield intended no harm.

Soon Scott found himself alongside a small circular table in the center of a round auditorium. The other pupils straggled in one by one and formed a circle around him.

"This is a little exercise we try, Scott," Dr. Edgefield explained. "I have a small plastic ball here. The object is to concentrate your mental faculties on the ball and move it from one side of the table to the other."

"It's easy, Scott," Grant declared. "It practically rolls if you breathe hard."

"Then why haven't you been able to move it?" Gigi asked.

Has anyone? Scott silently asked.

I have, Danny replied.

And me, David added sourly.

58

A series of piercing beeps lit up a nearby screen, and Dr. Edgefield scowled.

"Now you all know we don't allow telepathy during the exercises," the doctor scolded. "Danny, David, what have you to say?"

Only now did Scott take note of the small electronic devices both twins carried in their shirt pockets. A practiced eye could detect small glowing green lights that matched those on the monitor.

"We were talking about our tennis match this afternoon," Danny said. "Sorry, Doc."

"Let's have no more interference, yes?" Dr. Edgefield said, shifting his gaze from one student to another.

"No, Doc," they answered on cue.

"Now, Scott, focus on the ball," the doctor instructed. "See if you can move it."

Scott sighed. It was a child's game. Hadn't he studied with Tiaf, learned to deflect rock slides and mend cracks in dams? Scott was half tempted to bounce the little ball against Dr. Edgefield's nose!

"No luck?" the doctor asked. "Maybe Grant would like to try."

Scott stepped aside and allowed Grant to take his place. The younger boy rested his elbows on the table and concentrated on the ball. Scott watched in dismay as Grant tried with all his might to stir the ball into motion.

"Try harder, Grant," Dr. Edgefield urged.

"It's hard, Doc," Grant explained. "I can't seem to—"

"Remember what we've worked on," the doctor barked. "Focus. Breathe in and move that ball."

Scott watched as bubbles of sweat appeared on Grant's forehead. Couldn't the doc see Grant was trying? But Dr.

Edgefield wasn't watching Grant at all. He was watching Scott!

"You can do it," Gigi said, creeping closer to her cousin.

"Go for it, Grant!" Jay cried. As Grant strained to succeed, the others grew mute. Ivan turned his head away, and the boy twins appeared shaken. Only little Isabella objected.

"Doc, he can't do it," she observed.

Dr. Edgefield pretended not to hear.

"Give it up, Grant," Geoff said, edging his way over.

"I can do it!" Grant shouted.

Yes, you can, Scott told him. *Focus on the letters. Now picture the edge of the table. Move it, Grant.*

Scott didn't notice Dr. Edgefield or the lights flashing on the far wall. He concentrated instead on Grant. But the boy had given up.

"You do it, Scott!" Grant cried. "You do it!"

"Do show us, Scott," Dr. Edgefield said as he jotted down figures in a notebook.

Scott looked at Grant's exhausted face and then turned toward the doctor with rare hatred.

"You've got all the answers, don't you?" Scott asked, offering Grant a comforting pat on the back. Scott then glared at the ball. Plastic bubbled, and the ball melted into a red smear.

"Look at that!" Ivan shouted.

"Lordy!" Grant howled.

"There you are, Doc!" Geoff added, laughing as the doctor stepped back from Scott's glance. "That telekinetic enough for you?"

"I knew it!" Dr. Edgefield cried. "I saw it in his eyes."

60

"How did he do it?" Isabella asked. "Was he given a different implant?"

"He's got no scar," Grant explained. "No implant. It's natural talent."

"That's not possible," Ivan said, shrinking back from Scott's wild gaze. The others did likewise. Scott read fear and awe in their minds.

"So I've played your little game," Scott growled. "You okay, Grant?"

"Sort of dizzy," Grant confessed.

"Proud, Doc?" Scott asked.

"I do what's necessary," Dr. Edgefield replied.

"We all do," Scott said, adding a threatening gaze.

"I think it best if we move along now," Dr. Faulkner announced. "Why don't you children get ready for lunch. This afternoon we have a shape quiz and then recreation."

The others seemed to cheer a bit at this news. Scott remained frozen, though. Geoff and Grant finally pried his feet from the floor, hurried him to the corridor, and steered him to the cafeteria.

"You might want to check out your room," Geoff said, pausing outside the door. "They put you in Number Twelve, next to Jay and me."

"I'm across the hall two doors," Grant added. "With Ivan. The boy twins are on the other side of you."

"Strange they should leave Twelve empty, right in the middle of you," Scott declared.

He read unease and fear in their thoughts. It was clear Twelve hadn't always been unoccupied.

Scott stepped down the hall and washed his hands. He then rejoined his comrades for a light lunch before following Dr. Faulkner back to the auditorium. The others busied themselves guessing which shape the doctor held behind a dark screen. Scott watched the boy twins with interest. They were right half the time, but did no better. Grant picked twelve of fifteen.

Are you trying? Scott asked the twins. Neither answered, but they allowed Scott to scan their thoughts. Yes, they were doing their best.

After listening to Dr. Faulkner's appraisal of the test results, the students passed the remainder of the afternoon in a large gymlike room where some played tennis and others tossed a basketball at a hoop. Scott joined in only briefly. He didn't have the heart. Later Malin led them all to a basement pool, and Scott swam off some of his anger.

"You swim pretty well," Danny observed.

"My brother taught me," Scott answered without thinking.

"I didn't know you had one," David said, splashing over beside Scott. "Older or younger?"

"Younger," Scott replied. "He'd be thirteen now."

"He's gone, huh?" Danny asked. "Like our dad. Grant says you lived with an uncle. I guess your folks are gone, too."

"Yeah," Scott said, masking the truth. "We get along all right, though. I get to travel."

"We don't," David grumbled. "Ever."

"You went to the museum," Scott pointed out.

"To study old, dead things," Danny muttered. "When Doc brought us here, he talked like maybe we'd get to go into space or something. We don't. We just practice and practice. For what?"

"I don't know," Scott said, gazing nervously up at where the three doctors stared down. "But I may find out."

Scott made himself a promise to do just that. And after

supper and a video, he prepared to do some exploring. There were so many things he didn't understand. The answers he sought were certain to reside in Dr. Edgefield's office.

He waited for darkness to flood the building. Only the narrow corridors remained lit. Dr. Faulkner visited each room a little short of ten o'clock and contented herself that all was well. After bidding Scott a good night, she locked his door. Scott only grinned. No George remained to block the doorway, and as for the lock, it was a simple matter to twirl the cylinders and turn the doorknob.

Once out in the hall, Scott made his way slowly, cautiously down one corridor after another. He located an exit, but found it monitored by a video camera. Worse, a uniformed security guard manned a desk beside the door. Dr. Edgefield's name was stenciled on the door three feet beyond the guard.

As if that wasn't bad enough, there was a lot of activity down the corridor where the labs were located. Technicians and orderlies were prowling about. Twice Scott ducked into empty offices to dodge them. Once he passed ten whole minutes in an unused closet when George happened by.

So—they don't make it easy, do they? Scott asked himself.

While exploring, Scott made a puzzling discovery. Whenever he approached an outside wall, a strange buzzing tormented his ears. He'd always been troubled that he couldn't reach Tiaf within the Institute walls. What had Gigi said about it being difficult to read thoughts there?

The answer lay within the walls themselves. Scott was certain of it. Perhaps they were constructed of a dampening alloy. Tiaf had hinted such metals existed. Or maybe some sort of transmitter jammed the signals. Scott crept down the corridor and made his way back toward the dormitory wing. There was an outside wall in the shower room, and Scott selected that spot for his investigation. He switched on the light, then concentrated on the wall itself.

He was searching for something hidden, but the wall seemed to mask itself. He could not break down its elements. Worse, the humming in his head grew louder and louder. Finally sharp darts of pain tormented him, and he dropped to one knee. The noise wouldn't stop. It continued to grow in intensity.

"Scott, what're you doing in here?" Grant called as he opened the door.

"Help . . . me," Scott pleaded.

Little Grant raced over and dragged Scott back from the wall. Once they were five feet away, the buzzing ceased.

"That's pretty stupid," Grant scolded, helping Scott onto a bench. "It's dangerous to get near the barrier walls at night. Doc turns up the juice."

"Barrier walls?" Scott asked. "I don't understand."

"Nobody told you?" Grant asked, frowning. "It's simple, really. Your mind wanders sometimes when you're asleep, and Doc says when they first got here, some of the kids couldn't rest. All kinds of dreams were running through their heads, keeping them awake. That's when he had the barrier circuits put in the walls."

"In the outside walls?" Scott asked.

"Well, to begin with he had them put in the walls separating sleeping quarters. But sometimes outside thoughts interfered with our exercises, so he had the barriers put in the outside walls. They're strong enough to knock you out."

64

"How?" Scott asked.

"They put in three parallel circuits of high-energy electron streams. The surges jam our amplifiers, I guess you'd say. They also absorb something Doc calls zeta waves. Me, I've never even seen a zeta wave register. Beta and theta sure, and once the boy twins recorded a gamma transmission. Doc says zeta waves are the ultimate mental process. They should make it possible to teleport or even split time. Yeah, those mysterious zetas! Doc talks about them all the time, but it may just be imaginary. Like I said, none of us has ever managed anything close."

"You're sure about that, are you?" Scott asked, sensing Grant was masking something.

"We never talk about this," Grant said, quieting to a whisper. "There was a boy here two years ago. Zach."

"What happened to him?" Scott asked, gripping Grant's trembling shoulders.

"He had a lot of headaches. Heard strange sounds all the time. I heard he had a tumor of some kind. They operated, but he died. Scared us bad, I can tell you. I had nightmares for weeks."

"Do you remember anything about Zach, Grant?"

"Not much. He had really light-colored hair. Didn't talk much."

"You didn't get to know him well then?"

"No, he didn't really fit in. Geoff got here about the same time and made friends with everybody. Zach, well, he was just sort of confused all the time. He never remembered which door led where, and he was always staring out windows."

"Anything else?"

"Yeah, I think Doc was really disappointed when Zach died."

"Why was that?"

"Jay told me Zach registered on the zeta monitors. But I guess it was because of the clover."

"What clover?"

"He had a birthmark shaped like a clover. Almost like the one Danny and David have. Everybody who comes here gets checked for that sort of mark. It's really weird, but I think it's got to do with some family of telepaths."

Scott shuddered, and Grant recognized his friend's unease.

"Don't worry," the twelve-year-old said, mustering a grin. "That was a long time ago. He didn't stay in Room Twelve, either."

"Grant, don't tell anybody I was out here," Scott implored. "They locked me in, you see, and—"

"Oh, they lock me in sometimes, too," Grant said, laughing. "I guess they haven't figured out that telepaths can work locks, huh? I won't tell if you won't."

"That's a deal," Scott readily agreed.

Grant left after securing Scott's promise he'd stay clear of the barriers. Scott remained to study the walls from afar, though. And the closer he inspected the ceilings, mirrors, and floors, the heavier he frowned. There were wires everywhere. Worse, the Institute was crisscrossed with microphones and video cameras.

This whole place is one giant trap, Scott thought. *A mind trap! And I'm in it!*

7

Scott passed a restless night. Off and on he was shaken by nightmare images. Once he was caught in a mousetrap. Later he was an insect glued to a sheet of flypaper.

As if being trapped wasn't enough of a torment, Scott had an additional concern—Tiaf. What must the old man be thinking? How might he feel? As cut off and alone as Scott was, Tiaf was little better. What chances might he take? What risks might he undergo?

Scott was awake two hours before Dr. Edgefield unlocked the door and stepped inside the room.

"You didn't get much rest last night, did you?" the doctor asked. "The video monitors caught you taking a midnight stroll."

"Did they?" Scott asked. "Me? That would be a neat trick. I was locked in, remember?"

"I don't think a simple three-tumbler lock would be much of a challenge for a boy who can heal broken bones."

"Maybe not," Scott agreed. "But then such things aren't really possible."

"Of course not," Dr. Edgefield replied with a broad smile. "Only a fool or a scientist would admit the possibility."

"Which are you?" Scott asked.

"Perhaps both. Scott, I'm not the enemy."

"No, you're my friend. That's why you keep me caged like a guinea pig, why you refuse to let me go back to my uncle."

"It's necessary," the doctor argued. "We've only just begun to examine your talents."

"Aren't you afraid the next thing I melt might be you?"

"No, you couldn't do that. Not intentionally harm someone, I mean."

"I wouldn't be so sure. A cornered animal will fight!"

"He needn't. Scott, don't you realize how lucky it was for us both you happened to be at the park? For Grant, too. Where would you go?"

"My uncle—"

"Oh, yes, the mysterious uncle. Is there such a person? Look here."

The doctor drew a folded poster from his pocket and handed it to Scott. Once opened up, it revealed a photograph of Scott and a physical description.

"We've displayed them all over the county," Dr. Edgefield explained. "So far no one's called. So you see, where would we send you? With no one inquiring, all we could do is turn you over to social services. They'd scarcely know what to do with you."

"You let me go," Scott replied. "I'll find my uncle."

"If you were to contact him, have him come here . . ."

"You'd never let me leave," Scott said bitterly. "I can read your thoughts, remember? You'd only take him, too."

"Why would I do that?" the doctor asked.

An icy chill ran through Scott's insides as he realized Dr. Edgefield might not have known of Tiaf's talents. Well, Scott had made another mistake!

"Think over what I've said, Scott. It would be so much easier if you would cooperate."

"Like Zach did?" Scott asked. The words struck like darts. The doctor paled and stepped back. And in that one brief vulnerable moment Scott probed his mind and found many truths.

The doctor was still standing frozen beside the door when Grant popped his head in and greeted Scott.

"Doc?" the younger boy gasped in surprise.

"He just stopped by to unlock my door," Scott explained.

"Grab your clothes and come on then," Grant urged. "We have to hurry, or Ivan and Geoff will use all the hot water."

Scott collected his clothes and followed Grant to the shower room. Moments later a refreshing spray of water was clearing Scott's mind.

After breakfast Dr. Faulkner again conducted her students to the study cubicles. Dr. Thomas was waiting there with small boxes. He handed each person a box.

"Translation games," Grant grumbled. "Nobody's very good at these."

Scott took his box and found an empty cubicle. He opened the box and stared at a series of foreign symbols. Some were Greek letters. Others were Arabic. There was also a Chinese word and an American Indian pictograph.

"Try to form a sentence from them," Dr. Faulkner said, leaning over Scott's shoulder. "For example, what's this?"

She pointed to the pictograph. It clearly depicted a running horse, and he told her so.

"See there? It's not so hard. Concentrate on the words and see if their meaning becomes clear."

"And if it does?" he asked. "Maybe I speak Greek for all you know."

"Try these then," she said, placing a handful of runic-looking shapes before him. "I doubt you speak this language."

"Then how am I supposed to know what they mean?"

"The people who wrote these letters, or symbols, encoded them with a certain residual memory. So Dr. Edgefield believes. It's worked before. Ivan's translated whole boxes of Arabic and Chinese characters for us."

Scott tried to peer at the other students, but the cubicles were enclosed, and he could not. He set about making some sense of the Greek letters first. He knew them. The Arabic scrawl was far more challenging. The doctor was right, though. When he concentrated, a sort of meaning seemed to flash through his mind.

The last group of characters stirred his memory. He'd seen markings like that before—aboard ship. The writing was Antrian, familiar to him despite his lifelong habitation on Earth.

"Dr. Faulkner, where did these symbols come from?" Scott asked.

"I believe from rune stones in Scandinavia."

"That's not true," he said, gazing intently into her eyes.

"You're right," she confessed. "Dr. Edgefield discovered a book with strange writings. We've tried to translate it, but even the Army decoders were baffled. We had a boy here who made sense of whole passages, though, in spite of the fact that he'd never seen a line of it before."

"Zach," Scott said, sighing.

"No, that wasn't his name," she replied. "I don't think we tried Zach on these exercises. He was so frail, you see. I suppose you know we lost him."

"He died, you mean."

"Yes. It was a great loss. Even Dr. Edgefield was shaken, and I didn't believe he took anybody to heart. I was wrong to think so ill of him."

"Were you?" Scott asked. "You sure he wasn't upset at losing his prize guinea pig?"

"You misjudge us, Scott. This Institute, too. We help talented children discover themselves and develop their abilities. There's not another school in the country devoted to psi powers. We have children here who can communicate across vast areas without artificial means."

"What do you call surgical implants?"

"Yes, I suppose you have a point. Still, we've made great progress. And if we can break through in even one area—telekinesis, for example—it will be an achievement rivaling the discovery of the wheel."

Will it? Scott asked himself. He wondered.

He was still arranging the cryptic characters into nonsensical passages when Dr. Edgefield summoned him.

"Come along, Scott," Dr. Thomas called. "You're wanted in the lab."

"Lab?" Scott asked. "I thought this whole place was a lab!"

"Please, you're disturbing the others," Dr. Thomas scolded. "The Institute is a laboratory insofar as experimentation is concerned, but we also have specific chambers devoted to chemical and biological analysis."

"So what are you planning to do?" Scott asked. "Dissect me?"

"It's a thought," Dr. Edgefield declared, laughing as he stepped out from a nearby doorway. Scott observed that the man had regained his smiling self-assuredness. Scott failed to match the doctor's grin.

"This is the chemistry lab," Dr. Thomas explained as he ushered Scott inside. "We do spectrographic analysis, explore the use of chemicals as conductors of beta and theta waves."

"And as dampeners for zeta waves?" Scott asked.

"I suppose you learned that last night," Dr. Edgefield said, frowning. "I registered my first zeta readings in three years the day after you arrived, Scott. And again off and on since."

"Yeah?"

"I've made all sorts of vain attempts to replicate zeta transmissions. The wave length is so short, and the frequency so precise, that I have no trouble tracking them. But I can't seem to produce them as I can others."

"Is that why you brought me here?" Scott asked.

"Well, I would be delighted if you offered a brief show, of course. But you have been reluctant so far to show us much. I thought you might enjoy a demonstration of sorts. Dr. Thomas, bring the ring."

The ring, Scott thought. Unconsciously his fingers reached for the precious article. Dr. Thomas placed it on a clamp, then switched on a powerful light.

"Ah," Dr. Edgefield cried. "Look at the effect it has on light."

"Give me my ring!" Scott shouted frantically.

"Now try the ultraviolet," Dr. Edgefield suggested.

The ring swallowed purple light as a shark might gobble a tuna.

"Just look at the heat readings, Vic," Dr. Thomas declared. "Have you ever seen anything to match it?"

"Now the laser," Dr. Edgefield ordered.

"You have no right!" Scott pleaded. "You'll destroy it!"

"What does the ring do for you, Scott?" Dr. Thomas asked. "Is it a weapon? Do you communicate with it?"

"It was a gift," Scott insisted. "It's got a valuable emerald in the setting. Don't you understand? I don't have much of value. Just that ring."

"And the symbol inscribed on the stone?" Dr. Edgefield asked.

"It's very old. That's all I know. My parents might have understood more, but they're dead."

"Perhaps your uncle could tell us."

"I doubt he'd consider it a worthwhile use of his time," Scott declared. "Give it back to me."

"Soon, Scott," Dr. Edgefield promised. "But first . . ."

The laser flashed, sending an intense light beam into the ring. Immediately splinters of fiery light split off in every direction, boring through walls and disintegrating equipment. One split a pipe, and water sprayed everywhere.

"Switch it off!" Dr. Edgefield pleaded as beams ate into a filing cabinet and singed the papers inside. Dr. Thomas deactivated the laser, and the light ceased. What remained was a lab filled with chaos and shattered equipment.

"What happened?" a pair of orderlies cried as they appeared at the door. "Doc?"

"Get some men to plug that pipe and clean up all this glass," Dr. Edgefield ordered. "You all right, Edgar? Scott?"

Dr. Thomas nodded. Scott stared at the ring and scowled.

"I suspected as much," Dr. Edgefield said, nodding to himself. "It amplifies energy. Is that right, Scott?"

"Find your own answers," Scott barked.

"You've enjoyed certain liberties," Dr. Thomas pointed out. "We could order you confined again."

"No, let him return to the others," Dr. Edgefield commanded. "We have data to explore. And Scott needs some time to think."

Time to think? Scott asked himself. *No, it's time to act now. I have to get out of this place!*

8

After sharing lunch with the others, Scott feigned illness and returned to his room. He didn't stay there long. Instead, he made brief explorations of the various corridors, identifying each video monitor and security station. Soon he'd digested the plans of the Institute. What he didn't know yet was how to escape the security desks and electronic barriers.

At dinner he asked questions about the barrier walls. No one said much. When he spoke of the grounds outside, Grant shook his head in dismay.

"We had a break-in last year. After that Doc had a couple of guard dogs brought out. Big ones. You wouldn't want to be out there with them," Grant warned.

There's a tall fence, too, Danny related.

You can't go, David added. *We can talk to you. You can teach us so much.*

I can't stay, Scott told them. *I'm in danger here.*

He might have added that they all were, but he masked

those thoughts. No point in unsettling the others. Maybe later, with Tiaf's help . . .

Dr. Edgefield entered the cafeteria at that moment, and Scott froze.

Doc never comes in here, Gigi observed. Scott read similar surprise in the minds of the others. Ivan rose and offered the man a nearby chair.

"Thank you, Ivan," the doctor replied, sitting down. "I want to bring you all some good news. I've been speaking on the telephone with certain colleagues of mine. They've expressed great interest in our progress. A team of observers will be flying to Dallas early next week to witness some of our experiments. This is a great compliment to all of you!"

Scott watched the others tense. Moreover, he managed to skirt past Dr. Edgefield's defenses and tear fragments of unspoken truth from his mind. These visitors would include scientists, yes, but there was a team coming from the Air Force, too. And someone from a Project Starglow.

The doctor knew very much more, but he was a master at screening facts. He had to be, living among telepaths. Scott hungered to know, and he sensed similar feelings all around him.

It's time we had a look in that office, he told Gigi.

You'll be taking a big chance, she answered. *But I'll help.*

Dr. Edgefield spent half an hour recounting parapsychic triumphs, but Scott paid him little attention. Only when he announced they would have the evening to themselves did he take note.

"Care to have a go at us on the courts?" Geoff asked, motioning to Jay.

"I thought maybe you'd help us learn to swim," Danny said.

"I'll do that," Grant offered.

"Scott's not feeling very well, and I'm a bit tired," Gigi told Geoff. "You and Jay try singles."

"Maybe we can convince Nathan to play," Jay said. "Malin's on duty tonight. He'll grab a racket."

They turned and set off to locate the orderly. Ivan and Isabella began arguing over a video. Scott laughed and started toward his room. Danny and David blocked the path.

"Be careful," Danny advised. "I don't think Doc trusts you very much."

"He put you in Twelve," David added. "They monitor that room at all times."

"Thanks," Scott told the twins. Gigi then hooked his arm and dragged him along toward her room.

"Everything they said is true," she whispered. "Are you still determined to get inside that office?"

"I need my ring," Scott explained. "And I've got questions that need answers."

"Curiosity killed the cat, they say," she reminded him. "Doc has a mean side. We could wind up in real trouble."

"Maybe you shouldn't go."

"And you?"

"I can't be any worse off, Gigi. These people the doc told you about—I have a feeling they're coming to see me."

"I read that in Doc's mind. And more, Scott. You haven't told me everything, have you?"

"I don't dare," he answered.

"Come on," she urged him, leading the way down the corridor.

They moved like shadows, cautiously sidestepping around the video monitors and dodging the orderly's station. Once they neared the office, it was even more difficult. The security guard, after all, maintained his vigil just feet away.

"What now?" Gigi whispered.

"We need a diversion," he explained. "Like a broken window, maybe."

"You can't," she declared as Scott concentrated on the narrow windows on either side of the door. "They're high-density plastic. Not glass."

"All of them?" Scott asked.

"Every one. Doc replaced the glass panes when he installed the barrier wires."

"Wonderful," Scott grumbled. "We're sunk."

"No, not entirely," she said, clasping his arm a moment. Then she boldly walked up to the guard.

"You're not allowed here," the security man announced in a gruff voice.

"I'm sorry," Gigi replied. "It's just that I saw a strange man hanging around outside the video room. The little ones got kind of scared, and I promised to come down and tell you."

"Oh," the guard said, turning to gaze at his monitors. Scott sent a surge through the one covering the front of the Institute, and the screen blackened. Next the guard tried to switch on his radio, but Scott fused the transmission circuits.

"Sir?" Gigi asked, pretending fear as she pointed toward the door.

"He out there?" the guard asked. "I'd better take a look."

As the guard rushed outside, Gigi waved Scott toward Dr. Edgefield's office. He easily defeated the bolts, and they slipped inside.

"Any idea where it would be?" Scott asked as he made his way among file cabinets and bookshelves.

"He's got a safe behind that picture over there," she pointed out.

Scott tiptoed over to a large framed photograph of the Institute and slid it to one side, revealing a hidden combination dial. Scott concentrated on the dial and slowly turned it. One by one subtle clicks betrayed the combination, and Scott finally opened the safe drawer. Inside he found miscellaneous papers, a cash box, and assorted keys—but no ring.

"It was here, though," Scott said, as a vision of the ring inside the safe flashed through his mind.

"They probably have it in the lab," Gigi suggested. "I heard the equipment running when we passed."

"Well, so much for that plan. Let's have a look at the files."

They approached the wall of file cabinets cautiously, but the instant Scott touched the *C* drawer, a siren blasted the alarm.

"Oh, Lord!" Gigi cried, rushing toward the door. Scott followed. Seconds later two security men barged into the room and grabbed the intruders.

"Nice try," the one who had been watching the front door growled. "What did you do to my radio, anyway? And how'd you black out the monitor?"

"That would have been Scott's doing," Dr. Edgefield declared as he joined them. "You can generate some sort of electrical pulse, can't you, Scott?"

"It was me," Gigi declared.

"No, Griselda, I believe not. Gentlemen, escort her to

her room. See that she's locked in. And keep a guard on this door."

"Yes, sir," the guards said, dragging Gigi from the office.

"I underestimated you, Scott," the doctor said, frowning. "I suppose you came looking for the ring. I had it removed for safekeeping. What exactly am I going to do with you? You make a game of confinement. Perhaps you would suffer more through empathy. If I had Gigi punished, for instance . . ."

"Do what you want," Scott muttered. "I'll never cooperate. And I won't stay here, either."

"There's no way out," Dr. Edgefield insisted.

"Every chain has its weak link, Doc. I just have to find it."

"I don't believe you'll have much luck this time, Scott."

"Don't you go betting on it," Scott warned. "Once I'm outside, people are going to know about this place, what you do here!"

"Are they?" the doctor asked, laughing. "Why, you'll tell them, will you? Somehow I doubt that."

"Why?"

"Everybody has his secrets, Scott. Who would television be more interested in, you or me?"

Scott grew cold at the notion.

"You see?" the doctor went on. "Who's doing the hiding? My studies are reported in major journals. Next month we have a group of senators arriving for a tour."

"The other kids could tell."

"Tell? Tell what? I'm legal guardian of those children. They came here of their own free will. It's hardly a story to match that of a mystery boy who mends his own broken bones."

"But—"

"Perhaps we can talk more later, Scott," Dr. Edgefield said, motioning toward the corridor. "Just now I have some business to attend to. You can find your own way back, can't you? Or shall I send for George? He would likely enjoy standing outside your room again."

"Why are you doing this to me?"

"What am I doing, Scott?" Dr. Edgefield asked. "Searching? Discovering? It's a scientist's nature."

"It's got nothing to do with science and you know it," Scott growled as he turned toward the door. "You've got some notion of twisting and distorting life into a new being. You're wrong! I'll stop you!"

"Certainly you will," the doctor said, laughing as he watched Scott leave.

Scott wasn't finished, though. He hurried down the corridor to the dormitory wing, but a security guard barred Gigi's door, and he kept a watchful eye on Room Twelve, too. Scott sighed and stumbled into his room, momentarily defeated. He lay in his bed, thinking, for several hours. Then, just before midnight, he rose and made his way to the door.

"Where do you think you're going?" George demanded.

"Put you on guard duty after all, huh?" Scott asked, mustering a grin. "I'm just heading across the hall. You know, to the shower room."

"Go on," George grumbled.

Scott hurried over and darted inside the shower room. It was utterly deserted. He examined the place for monitors, found a single microphone near a bank of lights, and fused its circuits. He also deactivated a video monitor in the corner.

"Plastic windows, huh?" he whispered.

Keeping cautiously away from the barrier circuits, Scott focused every last ounce of energy on the windows. They seemed to glow red, then white. Suddenly they changed. He'd converted the whole window into a narrow plastic strip.

Now came the hard part. He knew approaching the barrier would bring him pain—maybe unbearable pain. But he had to try. Breathing deeply, he raced toward the gap. His head seemed to explode as he closed toward the opening, and for a moment he couldn't see. Somehow he managed to continue, though. He leaped through the gap, then rolled along the grassy lawn outside until he was free of the wall's pulsating torment.

"Now, Doc, figure this out," Scott said, reconstructing the window. It was the impossible escape!

Suddenly the shrill scream of a siren pierced the night air. Scott darted over behind an elm tree twenty feet short of a tall chain-link fence. He massaged his temples and fought to clear the ringing from his ears as he called out to Tiaf.

Are you there, old friend? Scott called frantically. *Hear me! Please hear me!*

Tiaf's anxious voice answered, *Where are you? Why haven't you returned?*

I'm in their hands, Scott explained. *The Earthers.*

Come back, Tiaf urged. *You're in great danger. I know that place. You'll find only suffering there.*

I know, Scott said. *But they have my ring. I have to get it back.*

The ring's nothing, Tiaf declared. *We can fashion another. You won't need it soon. For now, only think of the park. I'll meet you there with the ship.*

Yes, Tiaf, Scott agreed. But as he tried to concentrate, he was bathed in the brilliant glow of a bright floodlight. Two large dogs appeared, barking murderously as they bared their teeth.

I won't hurt you, Scott promised the animals. He received no like pledge in return.

Guards arrived next.

"I give up!" Scott shouted, throwing his arms in the air and freezing as the dogs encircled him.

I'll come for you, Tiaf offered.

No, old friend, this place is a trap! They'll take you, too. Scott! Tiaf screamed silently.

It's all right, Scott assured Tiaf as the guards escorted him back to the Institute. *They don't know what they're searching for—not yet, anyway. And I'll make certain they never do!*

They know already, Tiaf argued. *They have you!*

"Easy, boys," Dr. Edgefield said, stepping to Scott's side.

"Everything all right, Doc?" one of the guards called.

"Just fine, gentlemen," Dr. Edgefield replied, nudging Scott along. "I'll take it from here."

Scott stared helplessly at the men and formed a picture of the park in his mind. He tried with all his might to concentrate. He couldn't organize his thoughts, though, or overpower his terror. Always before he'd had the ring. Maybe he couldn't teleport without it. He wasn't strong enough yet. Perhaps he never would be!

"Come along now, Scott," the doctor said, gripping Scott's hand firmly. "Let's take a walk, shall we?"

"You seem to be making the decisions," Scott grumbled.

"Now, won't you tell me how you managed to get through the barrier wall? People don't simply pass through solid rock."

"Maybe I turned myself into a flea and crawled out."

"If you could have done that, you would have gone farther than the grounds. And without the ring, you're handicapped, aren't you? Does it allow you to teleport?"

Scott shuddered, and the doctor smiled.

"Is that it, Scott?"

"I'll tell you nothing," Scott answered.

"You needed to communicate. Is that it? You can't do it inside. The barriers make sure of that."

"You think you know everything, don't you?" Scott cried. "You have no notion at all. You're a poor confused fool who grasps at ideas and distorts them into nightmares. Leave me alone. Leave the others alone. Let us be what we are!"

"And just what are you?"

"Scott. Myself."

"George, help him along to his room," the doctor instructed when they approached the front door of the Institute.

"The barrier wires," Scott pleaded as his ears began to hum. Dr. Edgefield motioned, and the humming stopped. Once inside, the doctor reinstated the circuits, though, and Scott felt as caged in as before.

"You've caused everybody a lot of trouble," George grumbled as he led the way to Room Twelve. "Why don't you get with the program? Wish I had a place that'd give me bed and board, schooling and money besides, just for playing card games."

"I guess you think I'm pretty stupid, don't you, George?"

"You could say that," the orderly said, laughing.

"Ever been in jail, George? Ever been shut up in a room all by yourself?"

"This isn't even close to any jail, son. Not even close.

Now you get along inside there and stay put. Get yourself a good night's sleep. And no more adventures, huh?"

Scott only glared. Once the door was closed, he noticed a newly installed video camera. With a howl of frustration, he threw his shoe at the camera, knocking it askew.

"You haven't won yet, Doc!" Scott shouted.

Then he drew back the covers and fell into the bed. He didn't even bother undressing. He was suddenly and completely exhausted.

9

Scott drifted in and out of a nightmare-plagued sleep that night. He was haunted by familiar-looking faces, and voices seemed to whisper through his dreams.

"Help us," they called. "Save us!"

He was roused to consciousness by George's heavy hands.

"Time you got up," the orderly remarked. "Doc wants to see you. Let's get going."

"Before breakfast?" Scott asked, yawning wearily.

"Now!" George shouted, grabbing Scott's arms and pulling him from the bed. "He's waiting!"

Scott paused only long enough to tuck in his wrinkled shirt and step into his shoes. George then led him outside.

"Scott?" Grant called from his door.

"George, let go of him!" Gigi shouted.

The others soon gathered in the corridor, and Scott easily read their concern. He prayed they didn't discover his own fear. He hoped to hide that from everybody—Dr. Edgefield in particular.

"You shouldn't go by yourself," Danny suddenly declared,

stepping between his companions. "David and I'll go with you."

"You get along!" George ordered. "If Doc needs you, he'll send word."

Scott couldn't help but cheer when he read the twins' brave, determined minds. The two of them together didn't muster a hundred and fifty pounds, and the thought of those wisplike children defending him brought thoughts of David and Goliath to mind.

It's all right, Scott told the twins. *Stay with Gigi.*

There was something solid about her, after all. He noticed how even Geoff and Jay, taller and older, seemed to huddle near her.

"Let's go!" George yelled, giving Scott a push down the hall.

"I'm going," he said, turning angrily and staring hard at the orderly. "You keep your hands to yourself!"

George started to push again, but a burning glow in Scott's eyes gave him pause to reconsider. There were, after all, the shredded straps to remember.

Scott slowly walked down the corridor, then followed George's pointing finger down a side hall and along to a small examining room. Scott seemed to have a distant recollection of the place. Likely it was where they had treated his injuries following the accident.

"Hop up on the table there, Scott," Dr. Edgefield said in an almost cheerful tone.

"Why?" Scott asked.

"Oh, just say it's to humor me."

Scott sighed and climbed up onto the aluminum table. Dr. Faulkner walked over and gave him a reassuring tap on one shoulder. She then took his blood pressure and timed his pulse.

"You can't keep me here," Scott muttered angrily.

"Maybe after you hear what I have to say, you'll want to stay," Dr. Edgefield replied. "Dr. Thomas, bring in the files, won't you? It's best Scott see things for himself. I don't believe he trusts us much."

"Try at all," Scott countered. "Go ahead. Tell me some more lies."

"Oh, you can believe or not as you wish," Dr. Thomas said, shaking his head. "But I suspect you'll find these papers of interest. I did."

Scott probed the minds of the three doctors. He read no lies. Instead he found himself confronted by revelations he hadn't imagined.

Scott took the first file folder and opened it. Inside was a list of unexplained psychic phenomena. There were stories of men vanishing, formal case studies detailing predictions of natural disasters, even articles from medical journals speaking of beta and theta waves.

"So what's this supposed to prove?" Scott asked. "You know these things are possible."

"Here," Dr. Thomas said, handing Scott a thick file. Inside were detailed medical charts, X rays, even photographs.

"This is extraordinary medical evidence," Dr. Edgefield said, spreading the pictures and charts out on the table beside Scott. "Any of this appear familiar to you? Look at the birthmark, the one shaped like a clover. It's almost identical to the ones Danny and David have."

"And that means something?" Scott asked, shaking his head.

"Look at this X ray," Dr. Edgefield added. "The eyes. Notice anything peculiar? This subject has a dual lens structure. I've seen such a thing only rarely, and each time the patient possessed unusual brain patterns. We recorded beta and theta waves on a regular basis, and then, bingo, we nailed our first zeta reading."

"This boy was more than telepathic," Dr. Thomas went on to say. "He could move objects around a room. I once watched him juggle seven baseballs without using his hands. It was quite phenomenal."

"He was telepathic and telekinetic—both," Dr. Edgefield declared. "As you most assuredly are as well."

"Your eyes also have dual lenses," Dr. Faulkner noted. "I noticed that when we treated your injuries. It's what drew Dr. Edgefield's attention, that and your obvious advance knowledge of the accident. Once we interviewed Griselda, and she narrated your actions, it was clear you had had a precognitive episode."

"Have a look at these, Scott," Dr. Edgefield said, tossing a pile of newspaper clippings on the table. "Notice anything about them?"

Scott read a few. Each concerned a mysterious warning given by a stranger. Some went back seventy years. Others were recent, such as the report of a fourteen-year-old who had prevented a tragic accident in Wichita, Kansas.

"I thought you'd enjoy seeing that one," Dr. Thomas said. "Here's a drawing based on the witnesses' descriptions."

Scott stared at a pale, blond-haired boy who resembled him in every way. Why not? It *was* him!

"You gave us some conflicting information about your birth," Dr. Edgefield pointed out. "It's strange how a lie can lead to the truth, though. There were no peculiar events in Kansas on that date, but out west, in New Mexico, there was an unusual U.F.O. sighting. The U.S. Air Force found physical evidence of a type hitherto unknown. Moreover, they discovered a small child."

Scott shuddered as the doctor drew out a separate file and revealed the portrait of an infant.

"Notice the clover-shaped birthmark, Scott," Dr. Faulkner said with a smile. "Obviously, it was removed during the years the Air Force lost track of you, because there's no sign of it now."

Dr. Edgefield spread out an assortment of reports and photographs on the examination table.

"I could write a fair biography from this data," Dr. Thomas noted. "There's something I fail to comprehend, however. I have an autopsy report. This subject was killed in a bridge collapse a year back."

"Or was he?" Dr. Edgefield asked, holding up the newspaper story on the crash. Scott's freshman yearbook picture stared out from the yellowing page.

"You must possess an amazing ability to shape images in people's minds," Dr. Faulkner observed. "Over great distances, too. You needn't have feared discovery, you know. You weren't the first. We would have brought you here, given you a chance to polish your talents. And your parents and friends would have been spared the grief of your ruse."

"Stepparents, that is," Dr. Edgefield pointed out. "Your real parents were killed in the crash, I imagine. Where is it you come from, Scott? Alpha Centauri maybe? We know there are planets orbiting that star."

"It must be a considerable civilization," Dr. Thomas added, presenting Scott with a star atlas much like the one Tiaf had aboard the ship. "We can't make any sense of the language, but perhaps you can. Do you travel with others? Is this uncle of yours a visitor as well?"

"Where did you get that atlas?" Scott asked, trembling as he fingered the cold pages. A single name was written on the flyleaf: Tymor.

"There was another crash, Scott," Dr. Edgefield revealed. "Just after your own. This cylinder, if that's a correct term to use, survived in part. Some of the passengers eluded us, but we found some of the survivors."

"Three, all together," Dr. Faulkner said, taking over. "One was very young, like yourself, and he was placed in the care of a family."

"The others—well, let's show him the film," Dr. Edgefield suggested.

Dr. Thomas opened up a movie screen and placed it on a wall hook. He then brought out a movie projector and started up a film.

"We called them Tim and Jim," Dr. Faulkner said, swallowing a wave of emotion as a pair of boys appeared on the screen. They were twelve or thirteen, seemingly brothers, and both bore clover-shaped blotches on their bare shoulders. The film observed them communicating the identity of playing cards despite a lead barrier wall. They moved objects about quite freely.

"They were amazing," Dr. Edgefield commented. "I tested them for intelligence using Wexler and Stanford-Binet. The average I.Q. result registered 280."

"Tim," Scott muttered. "Tymor? He had the atlas, didn't he?"

"He told us he was training to be a navigator like his father," Dr. Thomas replied. "But as to how the ship functioned, or where it came from, the boys were mute."

"Where are they now?" Scott asked.

"That's a sad tale indeed," Dr. Edgefield began. "First of all you have to understand, Scott, that all this happened in a primitive age. We didn't know much, and people were afraid. E.S.P. was a novelty. Talk of men from outer space brought on panic and alarm. No one imagined the potential of those boys."

"One specialist asserted that they were Earth children carried off years before and raised elsewhere," Dr. Faulkner added. "The physical likeness was so great! Others argued the boys were human mutations, a leap forward. We, of course, knew better, but the Air Force supervised the investigations and had control of the subjects."

"Subjects?" Scott asked. "They weren't lab mice!"

"In a certain way they were," Dr. Thomas argued. "They were the clue to unraveling a mystery. It was determined that the first step to understanding their unusual capabilities was to examine the physiology of the process."

"No," Scott said, as his mind filled with a terrifying scream. He saw the body of Tymor, the older of the two, wheeled into an examination room. Doctors gathered around the body and prepared to administer a spinal tap. One gave the boy an injection, and a crisis ensued.

"We lost Tim," Dr. Faulkner said, wiping her eyes. "He had a reaction to medication."

"And the younger boy?" Scott asked.

"He stopped eating," Dr. Edgefield explained. "Withdrew completely."

"It broke my heart, watching Jimmy drift away, just dry up inside and melt before my eyes," Dr. Faulkner said. "And afterward, when the Air Force medical people conducted their precious autopsies, they discovered nothing!"

92

"The dual-lens eyes," Dr. Thomas reminded her.

"We knew about those already," Dr. Faulkner complained. "And we lost what chance we had to learn from them."

Scott took another file from Dr. Thomas. He read with horror a catalogue of organs, saw how a live entity with hope and spirit could be broken down into so many spare parts. And he recalled a nightmare he'd suffered that now was revealed to be fact.

"You had Zach, too," Scott told them.

"Yes, but he was like you, Scott," Dr. Faulkner declared. "Oh, his mind was much stronger. He emitted zeta waves the first day he was here. But he didn't know how or why, and he couldn't focus his energies."

"He was lonely," Scott said, reading her memories. "Like Jim. You isolated him, too. Why? He was little and confused. He needed help, and you subjected him to experiments! He died on you."

"He had a tumor," Dr. Thomas argued.

"That's what you told the others," Scott muttered. "Don't lie to me. I'm in your mind. I can read the truth there. He was too fragile, and scared, too. You hurried him the way you did Grant during that telekinesis experiment. Zach turned to you all for comfort, for understanding, but you were too busy studying him."

"No, Scott," Dr. Faulkner pleaded.

"Is that what lies ahead for me? For the others? Will you murder us all?"

"We're not barbarians," Dr. Edgefield insisted. "We only want answers."

"You won't find any," Scott warned. "Don't you have enough blood on your hands? Let me go!"

"There's not a chance of that," Dr. Edgefield declared. "We still have too many questions. And anyway, some gentlemen are on their way here from Washington. To see Scott Childers."

"You didn't even change your first name," Dr. Faulkner observed. "Nor the initial letter of your last name. Are you certain you didn't want to be traced, to return to your family?"

"If that was my plan, it didn't work out too well, did it?" Scott asked. "I suppose you told them?"

"That would hardly help things," Dr. Thomas explained. "We could scarcely tell them the son they buried was being held for interrogation in Dallas."

"Oh, is that why you're holding me?" Scott asked. "And here I thought it was so you could slice me open, study my parts!"

"He's too upset to continue," Dr. Faulkner announced. "Leave him some time to absorb this information. He'll respond then."

"Don't you bet on it!" Scott barked.

"Order him confined in a secure room then," Dr. Edgefield instructed. "Don't bother activating surveillance. He's taken a fair measure of delight in ruining expensive equipment."

"The video room should do," Dr. Faulkner declared. "The others will be busy with their lessons. Can he have breakfast in the cafeteria with them?"

"No, keep him isolated until we talk again. Let him calm down before he visits with the others."

Before I tell them they're in the hands of murderers, Scott thought. *I'll see they learn, though*, he promised himself. *And I'll see you stopped!*

94

10

Scott remained in the solitude of the video room for what seemed an eternity. Over and over again he saw the files, recalled the photographs, remembered faces that before had only been specters in his dreams.

They were my brothers, in a way, Scott thought. And as he considered the future, a terrible sense of dread crept over him. These men coming from Washington—what was their purpose? What of Grant and Gigi, Geoff and Jay, solemn little Nathan, mischievous Ivan and his quiet sister Isabella, the twins David and Danny?

Malin brought Scott a lunch tray. "Trashed that garbage they sent you," the orderly whispered. "Gigi smuggled this stuff off Granny Islington's table. Eat it all, Scott, else they'll hang me by my ears!"

"Thanks, Malin," Scott said, taking the tray.

"The others have their fingers crossed. Said to tell you."

Scott forced himself to grin. They would all need some luck, he suspected.

Scott gobbled every morsel of food on the plate. He'd

missed breakfast, and anxiety had produced a terrible hunger. He gazed in the mirror and took note of his hollow eyes and gaunt appearance. The life had seemingly been squeezed out of him. Tiaf had once explained the physical drain brought on by healing. Scott suspected he was suffering something even worse.

Keep it up, Scott, and you'll just dry up like Jim or Zach, he told himself. He hungered to tell Tiaf of the others, the boys who must also have been Antrian refugees. Moreover, he began to wonder if there weren't others like himself—perhaps the twins . . .

Malin reappeared then with instructions to return Scott to the lab.

"They got everybody else in there already," Malin explained. "Expecting some fancy tricks from you, or so the lady doc told Gigi."

Scott nodded and trudged along. Once at the lab, he followed Dr. Faulkner to one of three examining tables and sat on the cold aluminum top.

"Here," Dr. Edgefield said, strapping on a peculiar bonnet laced with wires. "Now, Scott, see if you can move this little truck across the floor."

Scott stared at the miniature vehicle. It was one of those radio-controlled toys, and the bonnet was supposed to translate Scott's energy into action. Scott scowled, folded his hands across his chest, and waited for the doctors to grow tired. It happened rather quickly.

"I'd hoped you would perhaps show the others some of your talents," Dr. Edgefield said as he removed the bonnet. "You didn't register a single zeta wave in the video room. This is quite a disappointment."

"Bet you can do it without the helmet, Scott," Grant called. "Show him!"

Scott shook his head defiantly, and Dr. Edgefield ordered Danny and David to climb atop the other tables. The doctor provided each with a similar hood, and David managed to slide the car halfway across the room. Danny sent it racing back, turned it through the doorway, and propelled it on down the corridor past a surprised technician.

"Well, that's more like it," Dr. Faulkner declared. "Weren't they great, gang?"

The others applauded cautiously. Then Dr. Edgefield chased Scott off the third table and placed a small stand in his place. On top of the stand the doctor laid Scott's ring.

"That's mine!" Scott shouted.

"Sit down," Dr. Thomas ordered, blocking Scott's path. "Do you want to return to isolation?"

"Keep still, Scott," Gigi warned. "He means it."

Scott stared hatefully at Dr. Thomas while Dr. Edgefield led David over to the ring.

"David, focus your attention on this ring. Then think of your room. Picture it exactly as it was this morning," the doctor continued. "Soon you will feel a warm glow."

"And then?" David asked, gazing back at the other students.

"You will go there," the doctor explained.

"He's going to teleport!" Ivan cried. "That'll be something to see!"

David concentrated hard, and Scott could read the excitement in the boy's thoughts. But inside the Institute, with its barrier circuits, it would take a powerful mind, even amplified by the emerald, to transport a body even fifty feet. David failed to budge.

"Danny, you try," Dr. Edgefield directed.

Danny repeated the exercise with equally feeble results.

"What are we doing wrong, Scott?" Dr. Edgefield asked. "Is the ring an individual thing? Won't it work for others?"

Scott suspected it would. Zach might have vanished in a flash. Tim or Jim would certainly have, for they were used to teleportation. The twins, for all their promise and enthusiasm, were not Antrians. Scott sensed that, and they read it in his thoughts.

"He's told them not to try!" Dr. Thomas accused. "Maybe Scott would be happier elsewhere. How would you enjoy a night or two in police custody, Scott?"

"I'd manage easily enough," Scott boasted.

"I fear he would," Dr. Edgefield told his colleagues. "Any other suggestions?"

"Scott could demonstrate for us," Gigi said.

Dr. Edgefield paled. He quickly snatched the ring and placed it securely in his shirt pocket.

"Return to your study cubicles," the doctor ordered. "See to it, Iris."

Dr. Faulkner gathered the students and formed a single file. She then led the way down the corridor. When they passed the recreation room, though, Grant pulled Scott inside, and Gigi followed. A minute later the twins darted in and closed the door.

"You have to tell us what's happening!" Gigi said, waving toward a small equipment closet. "Come on. They'll never find us in there."

"Forget our monitors?" Danny asked, pointing to the electronic device in his pocket.

"Toss them," Scott suggested.

98

"Can't," Grant explained. "If they're more than three inches from our hearts, they'll register on Doc's machines."

"I can take care of that," Scott boasted, gazing at each device in turn. The delicate circuits melted into a mass of copper wire and plastic relays. Scott then tossed all four monitors into a handy garbage can.

"Let's go," Gigi called, and the five of them slipped inside the deep closet, closed the door, and settled in among the volleyballs and tennis rackets.

"Well?" Grant asked.

"You know most of it, probably better than me," Scott told them. "About Zach, for instance."

"He didn't have a tumor?" Grant asked. "You mean—"

"You remember he had a birthmark on his shoulder shaped like a clover?" Scott asked.

"Sort of like the ones we have," David said.

"Like Dad's," Danny added.

"Your father had a mark like that?" Scott asked. "Clover shaped? You remember that?"

"Sure," David answered. "He rubbed it sometimes and gazed off at the stars. Mom used to say he was star touched. It's about all I remember of him."

"That's weird," Grant said, gazing at Gigi. "Grandma Henry had a mark like that."

"She did," Gigi agreed. "She was a strange old woman, always predicting things like earthquakes and floods."

"Was she right?" Scott asked.

"That's the thing," Grant said, trembling slightly. "Always."

"They wrote about her in the papers," Gigi explained. "People came around to ask her questions all the time. She ended up going off someplace by herself. California, I think, or Oregon."

"Dad knew things, too," Danny confessed. "I suppose it was precognition, come to think of it."

"He knew he was going to die," David said sadly. "How and when. We never told Mom, or anybody else before now. But he talked to us about going away."

"And he said growing up would be hard without a guide," Danny recalled, dropping his chin onto his chest. "We were just five. Two years later Doc talked to Mom, and we were dragged off here."

"It's almost the same story with me," Grant related. "Gigi was here already. My folks died, and my relatives were passing me around like a bad cold. Doc said I could come out here, be with my cousin Gigi, so I said, 'Sure.' "

"What's it all mean, Scott?" Danny asked. "And what's an Antrian?"

"What's Zhypos?" David added.

"Where did you hear those words?" Scott asked.

"We read them in your head," Danny said, exchanging an uneasy glance with his brother. "But they sound familiar."

"Zhypos was once a city on the planet Pyto," Scott explained. "In the Antrian star system, way out near the Orion Nebula. A great civilization thrived there, but the Antrian star exploded."

"Went nova?" Grant asked. "Did everybody die?"

"The Antrians were a strange race," Scott continued. "They appeared humanoid, but their minds had developed past those on Earth. For instance, many were telepathic. Nearly all, in fact. Some had even greater abilities. They were called seers. They could foresee events."

"Like the nova?" Danny asked.

"Exactly. Now, some seers had truly extraordinary powers. They could convert matter to other forms, change molecules, even move large objects. In fact, some even developed the ability to teleport themselves and objects across great distances. Seers guided spacecraft, in fact. They traveled through time and space."

"They came to Earth, then," Gigi concluded.

"Some did. Many tried to use their talents to reverse the deterioration of the Antrian star. Others went back in time to a safer age. And many chose to accept their fate and die with their sun."

"How can you tell an Antrian from a human, Scott?" Grant asked.

"I never knew before I came here. Now I think it has to do with the eyes. And they have a birthmark shaped like a clover."

"Dad?" Danny asked.

"And maybe our grandma too?" Grant cried.

"That explains a lot," David said, trembling slightly. "It's why we can move things around. Why we read people's thoughts."

"What about Geoff and Jay and Nate?" Grant said, scratching his head. "Ivan and Isabella?"

"They're what Doc thought we all were," Gigi said. "Humans with strong psi powers. Grant and I, we get our gift from Grandma Henry. You twins get yours from your father. But we're not seers, are we, Scott?"

"I'd guess your Earther ancestors contributed to your makeup too," he replied. "Don't feel cheated, Gigi. It's a gift of sorts. You can fit in."

"You're wrong," she complained. "We're different! And that's a hard thing to be."

"Hard?" Scott asked. "Sometimes it can be fatal."

"I didn't mean that," she objected. "It's just that I remember how it was at school. Everybody called me names and said that I was weird!"

"Stop that," he said, taking her hand and squeezing it. "You aren't little anymore. You know how to fit in."

"And what about us?" Danny asked. "Maybe we're not seers like Dad, but—"

"We're getting stronger," David broke in. "I could feel myself getting warm, staring at that ring. I think I might have been able to teleport."

"Inside this place?" Scott asked. "That's bad. Sooner or later they'll find a way to force you to do it. Probably when the visitors arrive from Washington."

"What about you, Scott?" Gigi asked. "Doc knows all about Antrians, doesn't he? What happened to your birthmark? Did you erase it like you healed your legs?"

"No, a doctor thought it might be a skin tumor," Scott explained. "He cut it out long ago. The scar healed itself."

"An Earth doctor, you mean," she said. He read a thousand questions in her mind. The others were likewise wondering. And so Scott opened himself up to them, allowed them to probe his recollections. As they explored the happier days when Scott had been just another average kid, with a mom and dad and brother, tears appeared in their eyes.

This Tiaf, will he come for you? Danny asked.

I pray not, Scott silently answered.

"You're the one Doc's been looking for," Gigi declared.

"Ever since Zach died, his thoughts have been full of you. And now he's got you."

"We have to get you away from here," Grant declared. "Before something happens to you, too."

"And what about you guys?" Scott asked, gazing at the pale faces of his companions in the dim light of the closet. "You're in danger too."

"Where would we go?" Gigi asked. "Mars?"

"I'm not alone," Scott reminded them. "Tiaf's near. He would help."

"It'll be dangerous," Gigi observed. "Especially now that Doc's on his guard. But what do you say? Shall we try?"

"Better cut Ivan in," Grant said, brightening. "Malin will help if he doesn't have to take too big a chance."

"Nathan's always playing with the communications circuits," Danny said, nudging his brother. "I'll bet the three of us could play a game or two."

"There's more involved than just getting me away," Scott warned. "I need my ring. And I read something in Dr. Edgefield's mind about other kids. He hasn't brought everyone here yet."

"He's got miles of files," Gigi said, frowning. "We'll have to get into that office again. This time we know about the alarm system, though."

"We'll tackle that," David boasted. "It's computerized. That's my favorite hobby, scrambling programs."

"You ought to know," Scott warned, "that they're sure to take all this very seriously."

"Yeah, we know," Danny said soberly. "But what else is there to do?"

David nodded his agreement.

"Grant, Gigi?" Scott asked.

"I remember Zach," she said, gripping Scott's hand. "We'll get you out of here."

"It's only fair," Grant added. "We got you in."

11

The plot was launched that same evening. After supper Grant drew Ivan aside, and they darted off to the rec room to play Ping-Pong. Actually their minds were elsewhere, dreaming up ways to bedevil Dr. Edgefield's security arrangements.

David and Danny escorted Nathan to the video room, where the three of them sat down at a computer terminal. In no time Nathan was tapping into the communications program, devising ways to sabotage the system.

Gigi and Isabella raided the laundry. Between them they sneaked a sheet and five towels past the watchful eyes of the night supervisor, Mrs. Wallace. Geoff and Jay meanwhile acquired a bottle of alcohol and some phosphorus from the chemistry lab.

Scott's job was to devise a way to bypass the barrier walls. They, after all, might prove as perilous as lead projectiles fired from a guard's pistol. It wasn't promising. Dr. Edgefield had thought of everything. If the electrical circuits were cut, a backup battery provided emergency power.

"Not immediately," Nathan explained when the conspirators met in the video room just before lights-out. "You've got maybe a ten-second delay. If we time it right, you might get out a door if you hurry."

"They'll be watching the doors," Gigi pointed out.

"No, they'll be busy with the fire," Ivan said, grinning. "Those towels will set off every fire alarm in the place, and the guards are sure to come running."

"Where will you set it?" Nathan asked.

"Where else?" Grant asked. "In the orderlies' lounge. You all know how George smokes in there. Well, his cigarettes won't be the only thing burning tomorrow."

"Why not tonight?" Gigi asked.

"They'll be edgy tonight," Nathan pointed out. "And we're tired. Besides, I need some time to play with the communications circuits. It's a complicated sequence, and we have to pull the plug on the power at the exact moment. Timing's the whole thing."

"Ten seconds isn't enough, though," Scott declared. "I'm not the only one going."

The boy twins glanced up, nodded soberly, and turned back to the computer.

"Gigi?" he asked.

She frowned heavily and turned to Grant.

"Listen," Jay said, "they're bound to evacuate the place if there's any threat of fire, aren't they?"

"I wouldn't bet on it," Grant replied. "Doc sure won't let anybody out till he sees the whole place going."

"We'll have to void the barrier wall," Scott said. "Is there a central control point for it?"

106

"Sure," Nathan said, shrugging his shoulders. "All the panels are in Doc's office. Now that's an easy place to get into, isn't it?"

"Not so hard," Gigi said, grinning. "Scott?"

"That's the best bet, then. We have to go there anyway."

"What?" Nathan cried.

"He's got my ring," Scott explained.

Nathan argued a moment about the risks of challenging the doctor directly, but in the end everything was agreed, and the plan took final form.

Scott had his first truly restful sleep in a week that night. His dreams were full of Tiaf, the ship, and the days of adventure and freedom that lay ahead.

He was up with the sun, and he joined in the foolish jousting and pranking in the shower room before breakfast. He filled two plates with food and ate every bite.

"I believe you've made up for yesterday," Granny announced.

"At least," Scott replied. "Can't ever tell when I'll get locked away in the video room again."

"Ah, Doc's made his peace with you, hasn't he?" she asked.

"I hope so," Scott said, sighing. "Isolation's hard on the soul."

Granny laughed and located a jelly turnover for him. Scott only barely stuffed it into his swollen belly.

He did his best to avoid the doctors that day. He'd had his confrontation. It was best to ease Dr. Edgefield's guard. Scott noticed the Institute's director paid him little mind, but one of the other doctors was never far away. And after dinner George took up a post outside Scott's door.

107

"Look," Grant whispered as he escorted Scott to Room Twelve.

"Don't worry," Scott answered. "I've got a trick or two up my sleeve."

He did indeed. For no sooner had George locked the door than Scott started on the tumblers. He cracked open the door and concentrated on George's simple mind. It was no trouble at all to implant a terrific weariness there, and in five minutes the big orderly was fast asleep.

"Time for the fire?" Grant whispered as he tiptoed past George and joined Scott.

"Soon as you can," Scott answered. "Tell Nate I'll expect the power cut at seven."

"That's only ten minutes," Grant warned. "Not much time."

"I know," Scott admitted. "But they'll barely have finished their own dinner and will be disorganized. George is here, so the orderlies' room should be empty. Okay?"

Grant nodded, then quietly made his way down the corridor toward the video room. Moments later Ivan scurried out that door and hurried to ignite the fire.

Scott sneaked past the other dormitory rooms and along toward the foyer that separated the laboratories from the study rooms. The Institute's main entrance was just to his left. Gigi stood waiting for him outside a storage closet, and she waved him inside.

"Anytime now," she whispered. "Be ready."

"Yeah, it's almost seven," Scott told her. "That's when the power goes off."

She gave him a nervous glance, but she never got the words out that she started to speak. The loud buzz of a smoke alarm split the air, and two sirens wailed immediately.

"Fire!" Ivan screamed.

"Fire!" Jay and Geoff echoed. "Help!"

"That's our cue," Scott said, stepping out of the closet, glancing up and down the corridor, then waving Gigi after him. They slipped past the abandoned security station and hurried to Dr. Edgefield's office. The door stood ajar, so Scott didn't hesitate. The room was empty, after all, and he closed the door to avoid interruptions.

"Find the control box," Scott said as he trotted to the safe and concentrated on the tumblers. In no time he had it open, but the ring proved missing.

"Over here, alongside the filing cabinets," Gigi called, pointing out a locked cabinet.

Scott turned his attention to the box. The padlock popped open with ease, and Scott examined the door for security wires. There were two circuits, and Scott fused them before opening it.

"I believe he's got wires and alarms in every foot of this place," Scott grumbled. "How's our time?"

"Two minutes," she answered.

Scott took a deep breath and counted down the seconds. Then the lights blinked out, a computer screen went dead, and Scott began tearing out switches right and left. As to the barrier wires, he located their junction with the control box and concentrated his energy on that spot. Bolts popped, and wires disintegrated. The power finally clicked back into force, but the barrier was dead. The circuits were broken.

Scott likewise deactivated the alarms protecting the files. As he opened the first drawer and began scanning the contents, he grew cold.

"Look at this!" Scott cried. "He's got records on hundreds of kids! See!"

Scott grabbed a handful and tossed them onto a nearby table. Gigi examined them, then raced over and tore open another drawer.

"Hundreds!" she screamed. "How can he do this?"

"Here's one with a birthmark," Scott said, shuddering as he glanced at files about children showing superior intellect, scoring high on intelligence tests, and demonstrating precocious talents.

"How does he get all this information?" Gigi asked. "And the photographs!"

"He had lots of help," Scott muttered.

"It's easy, I suppose," Gigi decided. "After all, don't parents want to hear their kids are smart, talented, and gifted beyond their years? I remember when Doc first came to our house. He was so free to praise, and generous, too. He took us all out to dinner, and he told Mom and Dad I'd get the best education, that I'd earn scholarship money for college. He paid them, too. And they all knew what a rough time I was having in school back then."

"I'm going to stop this," Scott said, stepping back from the files and angrily ripping one folder into shreds.

"What are you doing!" Dr. Edgefield shouted as he opened the door and confronted them. "Hey, give me some help here!"

"Shut up!" Scott howled as he concentrated on the files. In seconds they were a world of flame.

"Stop that!" the doctor demanded.

"Why?" Gigi asked. "So you can torment hundreds more?"

Dr. Edgefield reached for Gigi, but Scott tore into the

man's mind and screamed with fury. The doctor fell to the floor, clasping his ears.

"Stop, please," he gasped. "You're killing me!"

"Where's my ring?" Scott cried. "Give it to me or I swear I'll make you suffer like Tymor and Zach!"

"It's in the laboratory," Dr. Edgefield sobbed. "On the table!"

Scott stepped to the door and started to turn toward the lab, but Gigi held him back.

"No, Scott," she warned. "The fire!"

The burning files had spread to the office wall and thence to the adjacent laboratory. Chemicals bubbled and exploded. A wall of dense smoke poured out into the hall.

"No," Scott said, pounding his fist against the wall. "No!"

"Let's go," Gigi said, dragging him toward the door. Already Geoff and Jay were ushering the others outside, and Scott found himself carried along.

"The doctor," he finally managed to mumble. "I can't leave him in there."

"After all he's done?" she asked.

"Even then," Scott said, sighing. But before he could start back toward the Institute, George and Dr. Thomas helped Dr. Edgefield outside. Already ceiling sprinklers were at work on the blaze, and a fire truck arrived to help.

"We did a first-rate job of it, huh?" Grant asked as he skipped over. "Looks like you popped Doc's office, too."

"He had files," Scott explained. "Hundreds—"

"I can see it all," Grant said, frowning. "All."

"So what happens now?" Jay asked. "It won't take Doc long to come to his senses. Anybody who's going had better leave now."

111

"He's right," Gigi said, clutching Scott's arm. "He'll want you more than ever."

"You, too," Scott pointed out.

"No, I don't have any birthmark," she said, frowning. "I wish I did, because I think somehow you're going to a better place than the one I'll find."

"Come with me," Scott pleaded. "Gigi, please."

"Where? To another school where people can make fun of me? I'd like to go, Scott, but would it be better there?"

"Could it be worse?" Scott asked. "You saw some of those files. I'll get you somewhere."

"I suppose I could try things at home again," she said.

"Danny, David?" Scott called, turning to the twins.

"Gigi?" David said, shuddering.

"You two have to go," she declared. "Trust Scott to see you safe."

"Maybe we'll learn more about Antrians," Danny said.

"What about everyone else?" Scott asked. "Jay?"

"Geoff and I will see Nathan to his folks. Then we'll work things through. We've got money set aside, and we planned on early admission to college next fall anyway."

"Ivan and Isabella?"

"Nobody's waiting for us," Ivan responded.

"Or for me," Grant added.

"We'll find somebody," Scott promised, "and they won't have barrier walls and guard dogs, either."

"Better hurry," Geoff urged as he hurried over with Nathan. "There are police on the way."

The boys shook hands while Gigi and Isabella offered hugs.

"Don't forget me," Nathan said, and Scott offered a hand. Nathan, grinning from ear to ear, then firmly planted the

112

emerald ring in Scott's palm. "Didn't have anything better to do," Nathan explained. "I thought you might need it."

Scott slipped the ring onto his finger and nodded his gratitude. He then took Danny's shoulder in one hand and David's in the other.

"Gigi, Grant, Isabella, Ivan, huddle close," Scott urged. They complied, and Scott told them to read the picture he sketched in his mind.

"Breathe deeply and relax," Scott told them as he took a final glance at the Institute.

Tiaf? he called. *Tiaf, can you hear me?*

Young friend, come home, Tiaf answered.

I'm bringing company, Scott added as he concentrated on the familiar environs of the ship. Then, gripping the young twins tightly, encircling Gigi and Grant, and drawing Ivan and Isabella close, he stared hard at the bright-green sparkle of the emerald. There was a rush of wind, and they whirled through a great ebony void. Cold nothingness gripped them tightly, and they were gone.

12

Scott next opened his eyes in the control room of the ship. Danny and David stared in disbelief at the dials and screens.

"How?" Danny cried.

"Where?" David asked.

"You're among friends," Scott explained, turning toward Tiaf.

"You've been a long time gone," the old man said, stepping closer. "It was to have been a visit to the park."

"Yeah," Scott said, wrapping an arm around Tiaf and hugging the startled man.

"I—what is this—" Tiaf stammered as he regained his composure.

"An Earther habit," Scott explained. "Sort of a welcome home."

"Ah, I see," Tiaf said, recovering. "I missed you, too, Scott. And whom have you brought?"

"Danny and David," Scott explained. "This is Tiaf, twins.

114

He's a teacher. No, not like at the Institute. He's an Antrian."

"They know?" Tiaf asked.

"Show him," Scott said, and the boys opened their collars and exposed the reddish blotches on their shoulders.

"Your father was called Jyleb," Tiaf said, trembling slightly as he searched the twins' collective memory. "He, like Scott's mother, was a pupil of mine. I lamented his death."

"This is Gigi," Scott continued. "And her cousin Grant."

"Also of the blood, through their grandmother," Tiaf said. "And these two?"

"Ivan, Isabella, meet Tiaf," Scott said, nudging the two toward their rescuer. "I couldn't leave them—"

"No, of course not," Tiaf agreed.

"Where will we go?" Danny asked. "Traveling like Scott?"

"No, you have cousins among our people," Tiaf said, smiling. "Aunts and uncles. Jyleb was a twin himself. His brother lives yet."

"Where?" Scott asked.

"There's a place," Tiaf explained. "A refuge. Many of our people have gone there to live as Earthers. They would welcome these boys."

"And me?" Scott asked.

"Yes, you, too, hunger for a home," Tiaf said, sighing. "For family. But the colony excludes seers. You see, they blame them for what became of our world."

"We have certain talents," Danny confessed.

"Amplified twenty times," Tiaf said, resting a heavy hand on each boy's head. In the wink of an eye the old man extracted the devilish implants placed by Dr. Edgefield.

"You will be accepted now," Tiaf continued. "They don't bar telepaths, you see."

"And the others?" Scott asked, nodding toward his remaining four companions.

"Must make the choice," Tiaf answered. "They, too, would be welcomed," he added as he removed their implants. "Especially Aposia's grandchildren."

"That's Grandma Henry," Grant observed.

"Gigi?" Scott asked, half hoping she would insist on staying aboard the ship.

"The little ones will need some looking after," she answered.

"Will we ever see you again, Scott?" Danny asked.

"Maybe they'll permit a visit," Scott said hopefully. "Or perhaps you'd like to go with Tiaf and me on a trip."

"To Egypt?" Danny asked, grinning.

"Maybe we'll build a temple too," David added.

"Sure, why not?" Scott asked.

Tiaf conducted the twins to a pair of seats and strapped them in. Scott conducted the others to the narrow living quarters and saw them likewise belted in before taking his own place at Tiaf's elbow. Tiaf, satisfied all was in order, then sat in the pilot's chair. In seconds the ship whirred into motion, and in a flash they hurled themselves halfway across the continent.

"Where are we?" Scott asked, gazing at an image of roaring surf that took shape on the viewing screen. Nearby stood what appeared to be a small fishing village.

"The Earthers call it Oregon," Tiaf explained. "This town is the colony of which I spoke."

"Look, there's Dad!" Danny cried.

116

"No, Dad's twin," David said, sighing. "There are so many of them. Are they all Antrians?"

"Antrians and the offspring of Antrians," Tiaf told them. "Shall we go?"

Scott watched the screen as Tiaf and Gigi led the way toward the town. The people stared nervously at first, but they nodded as Tiaf spoke, and a tall blond man embraced Danny and David.

Good-bye Scott, they silently called.

Gigi and Grant were enveloped by a smiling woman in a blue dress. Ivan and Isabella found themselves adopted by a fisherman and his small wife. All waved toward the shiny metal cylinder as Tiaf headed back toward the ship.

Scott returned the farewell and waited for Tiaf.

"You were among Earthers a long time," Tiaf said as he returned to the pilot's chair. "Was it the adventure you hoped?"

"No, it was a nightmare," Scott confessed. "But good came of it."

Tiaf absorbed the events parading through Scott's mind and sighed.

"So many?" the old man asked. "So much pain."

"It might have been me had you not come," Scott said. "Tymor, the oldest was called. Another, too. And little Zach."

"They were beyond my reach," Tiaf said sadly. "When I came to this planet, I thought to save these Earthers from the destruction that came to our world. But who will save them from themselves?"

"Perhaps we will," Scott said hopefully. "Where shall we go next?"

"Anywhere," Tiaf said, clearing the screen. "Everywhere."

"Then we'd better get started," Scott said. "Onward!"

The screen began to fill with new images, and the ship whirred into motion. There was a flash, and another adventure began.

About the Author

Author G. CLIFTON WISLER notes: "*The Mind Trap* is a continuation of Scott Childers' story, begun in *The Antrian Messenger* and *The Seer*. The book grew out of the many letters I've received asking what might next happen to Scott. And it continues to deal with the difficulties faced by a young person who is 'different.' "

Mr. Wisler has written more than forty books for young people and adults. They include *The Raid; The Wolf's Tooth; Thunder on the Tennessee*, winner of the 1983 Western Writers award for Best Western Juvenile; and *Winter of the Wolf*. He lives in Plano, Texas.

Wisler G. Clifton

The Mind Trap   j34602

DATE DUE			